23AM

Declan Treanor

Declan Treanor

Copyright ©, Declan Treanor, 2025. All rights reserved. No part of this publication may be reproduced, stored in a retrieval system, or transmitted, in any form or by any means, electronic, mechanical, photocopying, recording or otherwise without prior consent of the author. You are allowed to think about the book after you have read it.

This is a work of fiction. Names, characters, businesses, places, events, locales, and incidents are either the products of the author's imagination or used in a fictitious manner. Any resemblance to actual persons, living or dead, or actual events is purely coincidental.

This book is dedicated to my dad, my mom, and my eldest sister.

Special thanks need to go to Leon, Jackie and all those at Solihull Writers Group for their help, support and advice. This book could have been so much better if I had listened to them.

Lastly, I would like to thank Anna, my long-suffering partner, and my boys Ben and Luke for bearing with me through all this.

Declan Treanor

23: Autumn's Mantra

Contents

Welcome to Secondworld 7

The Gatherers 9

Michael gets Gathered 11

Brown Bread 17

Cheerful Insanity 20

The Village 23

Boob-tube 30

Dirt Sticks to Sweat 34

Catney 38

4.54 billion years 43

Drinking with Victor 45

It's not dead 54

Hangover 55

Florence Ward 56

October 58

Dogs and other animals 60

Karl, the rest of his team, and the robots that he likes and who are his pets and that he has named 63

Mirror man 69

Welcome to Secondworld Carol 71

Transcendence 73

Dark Clouds 76

Hush 79

Murder a crow 83

Innocent..85

The Welcome Book..89

Rain..92

Drink again..94

New York crow...100

Chris Cook...101

The body..104

Teeth..106

The Garden Hermit..107

The Middle Kingdom Traditionalists.........................110

Market..113

The Twin..114

Not again...116

Innocent again...119

An Investigation...121

Dog...128

door to door...130

Luca Rossi...133

The call..139

The Falcon Man...140

The cabin...143

The Hidden..147

The sea..151

Autumn's Mantra...153

Prologue..154

Declan Treanor

Welcome to Secondworld

Michael lay on the pavement. He was in pain before, but not now. The ground was soft and the blood that had been collecting in his mouth was gone. The memory of a metallic taste lingered. Where were all the cars? What was going on? A blind panic was taking hold, or at least he thought it would be. When he looked for it, it was not there, instead only calmness akin to a dream. It was as if he was disconnected from his circumstance. He couldn't get a handle on why he felt so at ease. It was disconcerting how unbewildered he was.

He untangled the heap of him. People were walking past. One shot him a brief sympathetic smile, but most passed him without seeming concerned. They did see him. He knew this because they were altering their path to avoid stepping on him, but they did not seem overly perturbed by his presence. There were no looks of distain nor apprehension from the passersby. As Michael began to right himself and move from a lying position, he became aware that he was completely naked. He covered his modesty with his hands and looked around for a sign of reassurance or a sign that what he was experiencing was not really happening. Just then a woman, middle-aged and well groomed, locked eyes with Michael. She stopped in front of him and with hands placed on her knees, bowed forward. "Don't worry, just wait here, someone will be here to help you soon". She smiled warmly then walked off in the direction she had been travelling before. The comment, though offering no clarity to his situation, was surprisingly comforting. He remained in a seated position, knees up to his chest, and tried to recall the events that led him here.

He could remember the car crash moments before. He had been going to work. A brief slip in concentration? The impact, the strain on his body. The grinding noise of metal on metal. The world rotating outside the windscreen. A sudden pain. Blood. His own blood.

He was upside down, held partly in place by his seatbelt, partly in place by the distorted metal that was once his car. Michael had watched lazily as the pool of blood grew beneath him. He sensed himself ebbing from his body, draining away.

Declan Treanor

Michael was aware of sirens. Distant but approaching.

Was that then, or was this now? He snapped back into the present. He could hear the sirens clearly now. He turned his face to the direction of the noise, and into the sun. Squinting, he could make out a large figure moving purposefully toward him. "Hi, my names Karl and you've just died."

The Gatherers

Karl Blackstenius was a 'Gatherer' on secondworld. They were officially known as 'Midwives' but colloquially went by any number of names. 'The Gatherers', 'the Grabbers', 'the Gotchas'. For some reason there were a lot of 'G' words for the Midwives. They were also affectionately, though somewhat irreverently, known as the 'nuddy police'.

Karl liked being a Gatherer. No, he loved being a Gatherer. It was not necessarily the job that he loved, though he very much enjoyed his work, it was the sense of purpose the role brought with it. What was more important than welcoming others to their new life; their restart?

Before he died Karl had not felt that same sense of purpose.

Karl was broad and tall but stooped ever so slightly almost as if in apology for his height. The word 'bumbling' came to mind, maybe somewhat unfairly. He was not clumsy, but you could imagine this to be the case if he was required to move at any speed other than lumbering. He operated his body like a proficient, but newly qualified excavator driver; sure of the controls but not able to work them without dedicated concentration.

If Karl possessed more confidence, he could have been a majestic figure. A more confident man would shave the thinning hair that perched atop his head in a manner devoid of anything that could be described as a hairstyle. A more confident man would replace the hesitant stutter in his smile with a gaze that exuded self-assurance. A more competent man would be able to feed himself rather than his shirt.

But he was kind, or at least tried to be.

Karl's job was crystal clear—find them, pick them up, contain them, hand them a pamphlet, and explain what had happened. It was a routine task, devoid of ambiguity. The final step, the drop-off, hinged on pre-determined data. Most cases went smoothly, heading straight to processing, but the flagged ones were a potential source of trouble. The parameters of his role left little room for nuance. Karl liked that. He also liked that he could be chatty. He liked being chatty but found that sometimes others did not share his enthusiasm for this. The ones he picked up did. They were very receptive. A captive audience. Yes, they were literally captive, but it was more than that. They did not have a clue what was going on and Karl could explain it all. Moreover, it was his job to explain it all.

He could not be told he was talking too much: it was his job. He could not be told he was interrupting; it was his job. He could not be informed that others need to be included in the conversation; that the conversation had moved on or that the topic he had chosen was not of interest to the group. Eyes did not glaze over, nor were they rolled. People drifted in and out of giving him their full attention, but this was them being lost in thought or processing. Not because they were uninterested in what Karl had to say. For the most part, and for that period of time they were with him, Karl had their upmost attention.

After the Secondborn had become acclimatised it was different. When he met those same people later, they were less interested in what he had to say. Stilted, staid conversations; pregnant pauses; imagined impending schedules, 'I would stop but I'm on my way to…'. A few polite words then the inevitable 'Well, I should let you get on.' Responses that they were not keeping him, and that he had all the time in the world, were either dismissed or ignored.

Karl wasn't sure why people did not want to be with him. No, that was wrong. He knew what he was doing wrong but didn't know how to do it right. The awkward silences were palpable. He could taste them, could feel them in his throat, feel them trickle down the back of his neck. Like a diving bell, each moment that passed the pressure increased.

In his previous life it was the loneliness that killed him. It was not dramatic. It was a slow meandering death. That subtle self-neglect over an extended period of time. Decades of solitude.

Karl awaited Michael's arrival with the anticipation of someone completely ignorant of the fact.

Michael gets Gathered

"So, fellow being, can I ask your name please?" Karl led that way. He always did given half the chance. The 'fellow being' part was not in the handbook. When asked about why he did this, as would happen from time-to-time, Karl asserted that saying 'fellow being' was not gender specific, was unlikely to offend and caught the newcomer off-guard, making them more likely to give up their correct name. Karl had no evidence for this claim and would admit tacitly to himself, and no one else, that he just liked saying it.

"Michael." Michael said.
"Michael what?" Karl asked as he handed Michael a government issue coverall.
"Michael Stacey." Michael Stacey said. "Where am I?"
"Like I said, you sir are dead. Let's get you dressed and in the van." Karl offered Michael an arm to steady himself while two of his colleagues held up sheets to protect what was left of Michael's dignity.

When dressed Karl ushered Michael to the small white truck that the team had arrived in. The vehicle was nearly as tall as it was wide and gave the impression of instability. A child's interpretation of an ambulance. A milk float with ideas above its station. It had a light bar on its roof and the letters 'SMID' on the side panel. The sliding door on the side of the truck was already open. Michael was shown to a seat and encouraged to fasten his seatbelt. Karl sat in the seat beside Michael whilst the other members of the team filled the rest of the unoccupied seats.

Once Karl had fastened his seatbelt he began to speak again. "You may feel a little Swiss-cheesy at first. It's the brain reconfiguring itself. Firstly, it's a bit of a shock to the system, being flung into this existence I mean. Some can be a bit fragile. Takes them a moment. Did you have any neurological problems before, coz those go. Can take a bit of adjustment that. Some people with dementia can be confused that they are no longer confused. Now that's some roller coaster, emotionally speaking of course, not literally. It's sweet really, and they adjust pretty quickly. It's like a fog lifting, or so they say." Karl took half a breath.

Declan Treanor

"So, as I was saying. You're dead. Or at least you died. I know I have said this a few times, but they say that is the best thing to do; to tell you straight away and then keep repeating it. We've tried other ways, other than being blunt, but it didn't work. You probably have some questions but best you leave these until the end as I'm going to give you a fair bit of information. We are not expecting you to remember it all, but we are told you are likely to recall about 78%."

Karl took a small notebook from his chest pocket and turned to the required page. "No, this is not heaven, hell, purgatory, Jannah, Jahannam, Hades, Valhalla, Mictlan, Tlalocan, or any other connotation of religious afterlife, so far as we can ascertain. Also, you are not a God." On saying 'as far as we can ascertain' Karl raised one eyebrow. This was a practised routine which Karl deemed to be fitting. Michael let Karl's words wash over him as he watched the scenery pass the window. The scenery alien but somehow familiar.

"You are now being taken for 'processing'. This is where we will gather more information about you and your death. At this stage we are slightly restricted in what we can say to you" stated Karl before preceding to tell Michael everything.

"We call this place secondworld. Everyone who dies comes here. The next big shock. You will be here for 23 years and then you will die again. Take a moment." Karl took a moment. Michael turned to look at Karl after finally registering what had been said, his mouth opened but no words formed. "No, we do not know if there is another world after here." Karl continued.

"You will be allocated some modest accommodation. Following processing we will take you to your new home. If you have friends or relatives that have died in the past 23 years we can help you contact them. Please consider who you may wish to contact, they will ask you this in processing."

"Yes, everyone arrives here naked. Please do not be alarmed if your physical appearance has altered in any way. Has your physical appearance altered in any way?" Michael thought for a moment what that could mean and decided that it did not refer to him. He shook his head. Karl handed Michael a leaflet. "This has lots of information. We give you the leaflet at the end, so you are listening and not reading."

The title of the leaflet read 'You're Dead- So Now What?'

-

The steroided milk float squealed and bounced its way into the grounds of the Processing Hub. Karl continued to bark through his list of 'essential information'. The vehicle lurched through the courtyard past a fleet of Gatherer trucks that had been left to charge whilst the others were out on patrol.

The building was a vast concrete block and would have been considered bleak if it wasn't for the window boxes and hanging baskets that adorned the facia. Some were the most glorious bouquets of vibrant flowers, but some it seemed were housing produce. Michael caught glimpses of this through the trucks window but could not quite crane his neck enough to see the full extent of the building's height. A roller shutter announced its presence with a squeal. The truck entered an enclosed bay and came to an unceremonious halt. They waited for the roller shutter to close before alighting the vehicle. Karl led the way, talking all the time with the self-assuredness of an estate agent. "This is the Processing Hub. This particular iteration of the building was constructed in 1974. We will take the central staircase where you will meet one of our Processing Officers or P.O's as they are also known."

Michael was ushered into the room. A room too large for its occupant. The P.O. was sitting at a small table, positioned centrally in the office. There were chairs either side of the table, one occupied by the P.O., one free for the subject of processing. A small monitor and keyboard sat atop the table and a large diameter cable, about the size of a drainpipe, protruded from the monitor and ran to an internal wall where it disappeared into the blockwork.

"Good morning, please sit". The man gestured to the empty chair in front of his desk. "My name is Pearson, and I will be processing you today. I am sure the Midwives have given you some details of what has happened to you, so if you don't mind, I would like to start with some questions." He turned to Karl who was waiting expectantly "You may go."

"Thank you, sir" Karl replied, "Best of luck Michael, I hope everything goes well."

"Thank you." Was all Michael could muster at this time.

Pearson was thin with sharp features. Michael didn't quite understand his reasoning but felt Pearson's face was lacking something. There was an echo of something that used to be.

Pearson attended the laborious task of the interview. Name, date of birth, place of birth, gender, religion, the list went on. Data, data, data. This was essential to the smooth running of secondworld. Family members, mode of death. Were you married, were you employed, were you murdered? Is there anything that you would like to confess? This question was mandatory and provided some surprisingly candid responses over the years. People wanting to redress an imbalance, wanting to right a wrong, wanting to start anew.

All answers were logged on the desktop. After what seemed like an age Pearson made a statement rather than asking a question "According to our records, all being well, you will die again in 2047. Here is your date stamp." Pearson then lent across the desk and, without any forewarning, pushed a metal contraption onto Michael's forearm. Michael had no idea where the contraption had materialised from as he had not noticed it before, and the room was so very sparce. He frowned at Pearson then looked down at his arm. '08:47hrs -25/09/2047'. Looking at the number, it didn't seem that far away.

"Leap days have been accounted for. There are a few other essentials you need to know. You will be issued with food and lodging; these are free of charge. In your apartment you will find a welcome book with lots more information about secondworld, or there are some quite adequate documentaries available on the 'boob-tube'. You are currently resident in the Kingdom. The geography and history of this region is available via the aforementioned routes."

As the man continued to impart knowledge on various topics Michael became lost in his own thoughts. 'What was Darren doing now?' 'Did his mother know?' He just zoned back in to hear a warning about suicide cults and though he felt this may have been important he also felt it rude to interrupt.

Pearson conveyed some of the most fascinating information known to man in the most mundane, monosyllabic fashion so as to render it dull. "There are some that say they can speak to the 'other side', as in the side you just came from. Clairvoyants. If you were reserved about their validity prior to your firstdeath feel free to continue with your reservations. If you believed in them prior, I would advise you check the extensive records of these charlatans being exposed. It is very difficult to argue that you had previously made contact with a dead relative, when said dead relative is in the room being questioned about it."

Pearson continued "We hope that you will wish to be an active participant in the community, but there is no obligation to do so."

"You may feel out-of-sorts for a period of time. Don't worry you will soon acclimatise."

As he absentmindedly shook the man's hand a thought occurred to Michael. Pearson's face should have been furnished with spectacles.

Michael was collected by a different team of Midwives. "We will take you to your assigned home." They trundled along in silence while Michael continued to process the day. As they travelled the sun began to set though the air remained warm. The hues of the setting sun turned to dusk. It was getting dark as they pulled up. He was shown to the front door and given a key. The man waited for him to open the door then bid him a good night.

-

The apartment allocated to Michael was neat; compact but well set out. The short hall opened out to the living area. There was a sofa and an armchair pointed in the general direction of what looked like an old 80's television, a thing of substance rather than the thin but large iterations of the previous world. A set of patio doors were positioned to the right of the room with a tub chair set to one side. A chrome hooded lamp arched over the chair waiting to illuminate the space for reading. To the left a small dining table sat just before the open kitchen. Two further doors behind led to the bedroom and the bathroom. Moderate yet stylish.

This was a standard starter accommodation for a single fatality. If a new fatality had any family that had died before them, an application for joint accommodation could be made. Michael did not. Not any immediate family anyway. The majority of his nearest and dearest were still on world-one. There were some friends that he could look up, some family he felt obligated to look in on, and some others that he would have to do the maths on. Even if they did hit the 23-year bracket there was no guarantee that they were still here. They could have moved abroad or simply befallen an accident. He would look them up tomorrow, now he was tired.

His dad had died when he was young, more than 23 years ago. When he had first thought this thought it had tapped him on the shoulder. Since then, it had intermittently poked and prodded at him, delving a bit deeper each time. It was beginning to feel like the opening of an old wound.

He was suddenly extremely tired. He went into the bedroom and turned on the bedside lamp. Michael opened a window. The night was warm, but the open window offered a cool breeze. He would explore the local area tomorrow, now he just needed sleep. As he prepared for bed, he could hear soft guitar playing. The music continued and when he finally got into bed he was serenaded to sleep.

Brown Bread

Pouring his morning coffee, Michael had time to reflect on the events of the previous day. He could remember rolling out of bed around seven o'clock and ambling to the bathroom where he took care of his excretions and ablutions.

As Michael was coming down the stairs Darren, his husband, was coming through the door. Darren was an A&E nurse and regularly worked the night shift. There was a brief exchange before Darren, stupefied by lack of sleep, lumbered his way upstairs to prepare for slumber. Michael now chastised himself for not holding Darren longer, for not giving his full attention, for not saying goodnight properly. This was the last time he would see Darren and it amounted to a few ill-formed words, some grunts, and a peck goodnight. If only he had known. Michael replayed the last exchange again. He wondered how Darren had taken the news and wondered what Darren was doing right now. Languishing for a moment longer Michael then tore himself away from the thought. It was still too raw.

Brown Bread.
The morning of the crash Michael had taken two slices out of the bread bin and put them in the toaster. This was 38 minutes before his death.

Toast.
As it popped Michael had 36 minutes left. Before buttering he threw the toast in the freezer, just a few seconds to cool it right down. He was treating himself to pate this morning and the only way to have pate on toast was to cool it down first. People who did not do this were foolish. With pate you needed a crunch, you needed the toast to have the strength to hold the weight of the spreadable meat. It also had the advantage of not melting the butter, that way you could really slather it on.
27 minutes.

Belly up.
As Michael left the house the dog exposed its belly for one final rub. It occurred to him now that his final goodbye to the dog was more affectionate than his goodbye to his husband.

On the way out he hesitated in the doorframe, the feeling he had forgotten something came over him. Elusive. It escaped him. Had his keys, had his wallet, his phone, his case. "It couldn't have been important" he had remembered thinking. If only he had gone back into the house, delayed his journey even by a few moments. It could have changed everything.

19 minutes and he was in the car.

Whilst waiting at the roundabout his mind wandered. What would happen if he just pulled out into the traffic? The imagery of cars colliding vied with the imagery of them screeching to a halt just in time. The chances were that he would make it across without incident, leaving nothing but angered drivers in his wake. At least they would have a story to tell when they got to work- 'this idiot, God knows what he was thinking, just pulled straight out...'. He opted to manoeuvre the roundabout appropriately.

At the next junction, again he imagined a crash. A car going right into the side of him. 'T-bone', that was the name given to that kind of accident. Was there a T-bone in 'Grease'? He knew the gang was called the T-birds, but he thought one of the members of the gang (if that terminology was fitting) was called T-bone. Were they, or was he misremembering? He would look it up when he got home. Was that a gap? Could he make that one? He made the gap and continued his journey. As he approached the motorway junction 'Hopelessly Devoted to You' started to play on the radio. Michael felt somewhat nauseous. He could feel the bile rising in his throat.

Michael hated coincidences. He tried a brief exercise in rationalisation. He was half listening to the radio when he was waiting for the gap. They could have announced that they were going to play the song before he began to think of the film, a half-listening mind presented a subliminal Grease reference. Was that it? Is that what happened?

There are coincidences of course. Michael didn't believe this. He felt a twist in his stomach again. If there were no such things as coincidence, then why do we have the word? His mouth felt wet. The word 'unicorn' came to mind.

If he was part of some big conspiracy type scenario – what was the point?

11 minutes.

Michael found himself on the motorway. Initially the traffic was the usual sluggish crawl but soon began to pick up speed. He undertook someone doing 60mph in the fast lane. He imagined their protestations about the Highway Code and that you should not undertake. "Well, you can in slow moving traffic, and you're slow-moving traffic," he said to no one in particular "and you should keep left unless you're overtaking". He said the latter part in his head. "Can't obey one rule and ignore others."

He changed lane. The indicator ticked away his final moments; tocked them away.

The hum of the engine and the rhythmic whir of tires against the road formed a familiar melody as he drove, lost in his thoughts. Michael's eyelids grew heavier. He fought to stay awake, but exhaustion won the battle. He momentarily lost consciousness.

That was right. He remembered now. Right before the crash he had fallen asleep. No, not fallen asleep, had passed out. Jesus, how had he forgotten that?

The pain. The blood. The End.

0 minutes.

He went the way of all flesh. Shuffled off that mortal coil.

Cheerful Insanity

Michael switched on the 'boob-tube'. This was common parlance in secondworld. Nobody said television, telly, or TV for very long. You say boob-tube a couple of times and it sticks. He wasn't sure what he was expecting. The films were the most fascinating. Lots of remakes, no change there, but who wouldn't want to see James Dean as James Bond? John Belushi in 'The Blues Brothers' with Hendrix as Elwood. Jim Morrison in Apocalypse now, in the Marlon Brando role. How does anyone get anything done? Marilyn Monroe in Halloween. Stan Laurel as Scarface!? That's got to be a parody. Surely, he would have been too old for that role by that stage!?, not that age was the only issue with this. Michael needed to create a list. He switched it off again. He needed something to eat.

On the countertop there sat the 'Welcome Book' with three coins placed to the side. When Pearson had mentioned it, Michael had imagined the book to be similar to something you would find in a guesthouse. This was an encyclopaedia. Michael had surprised himself by not looking at this yet. A part of him wondered whether he wanted to hold onto the mystery on this world a little longer. He vowed to take some time to look through these later in the week. Next to the book and the coins there were a series of cards with writing on them, and hand drawn pictures of food. This is what he was after. He picked them up. They were recipes, seven altogether. He shuffled through them. Was it breakfast? Was it lunch? He scanned through the recipe cards and his stomach dictated that it was lunch. Pan fried chicken livers with fondant potatoes.

He opened the lower cupboard drawer, and on his first attempt located the frying pans. He took the livers out of the fridge. Naturally, all the ingredients needed were provided. He trimmed the livers before splitting them into lobes. He was instructed to soak the livers in milk first, he had cooked liver before and had never heard of this but thought he would give it a go. You only live once. While the livers soaked, he prepped his potatoes. It seemed a lot of trouble to go to for one person, but he still felt it worthwhile. There was something about this new life that made room for indulgence. Was this indulgence, or was it the art of doing something properly? Peeled and sliced, the potatoes sizzled as they were placed in the pan, the butter spat in revolt at these newcomers and proffered glancing shots at the retreating fingers.

To his right a window was set. This looked out across the back alley that ran parallel to the lower courtyards. It lacked the boisterousness of the front balcony vista but was not without interest. A stooped figure in a large blood red coat shuffled its way through the passage, stopping intermittently to examine the progress of the vegetable growth from the different varieties available to harvest from the gardens. A bike cheerfully rung its bell to alert the pedestrian as it zipped past.

Michael absent-mindedly looked around the flat as he poured in the stock. The violent protestations from the pan calmed. Music. That's what was needed. He looked first to the 'boob-tube' but as he scanned the home, he could see a device built into the bookcase that looked very much like a radio. He went over to examine it and found that his initial suspicion was correct. He switched it on and adjusted the scanner until he found something agreeable. He thought he may need to invest in some form of player, although he had no idea whether these were available or how he would go about getting hold of one if they were. He still had a lot to learn, and things that he would need to circumnavigate, but this did not seem like a hostile environment. Far from it. He felt at home here and thought that he had never felt as comfortable. Anywhere. Ever. He scanned his memory. Was the overall feeling of wellbeing a temporary state, a side-effect of cheating death? Would it fade away once the fridge was empty?

'The Cheerful Insanity of Giles, Giles and Fripp' played in the background. He recognised the group but not the song. Their sound was unmistakable, but he must have been mistaken. He thought about that for a moment and reasoned that he could not have been listening to 'The Cheerful Insanity of Giles, Giles and Fripp', they were all still alive, at least he thought they were, it would have to be imitation, a facsimile. Someone who missed the music and decided to repeat it. Had they died? Even if they had died, it would still be a replica. Not quite the original. The voices would be older, the marks not quite the same, a beat hit that had been missed before, a subtle but noticeable difference. A cover version by the same artist. The live version. The dead version?

Declan Treanor

His attention moved again to his lunch. He would eat and then explore the village.

The Village

Michael had been placed in Nesfield-upon-Hean. This was in the most part due to the location of his death. He would be able to request a transfer, if he so wished, but it was the responsibility of the Processing Hub to allocate the initial accommodation. Michael died on the motorway and the village was close by. Many people opted, at least in the short-term, to return to the area they lived prior to their death. It was unlikely that someone would be able to transfer to their pre-death home, as this would likely already be occupied or may be deemed too large for their needs. It did happen from time-to-time, principally when whole families passed at the same time. The occupying tenants would be asked to vacate and would usually do so with minimal fuss.

Donning his standard issue clothing; a plain grey t-shirt, some navy-blue utility trousers and light brown desert boots, Michael got ready to leave the apartment. The shoes were the correct size he had declared at processing; the trousers were somewhat slimmer, but then again, he noticed, so was he. Michael adjusted them to fit better. When dressed he picked up his front door key and looked around. There was the feeling that he was forgetting something but rightly reasoned it was the muscle memory of picking up his wallet and mobile phone. Of course, he had no wallet nor mobile phone.

Michael could have had a mobile phone if he so wished, though a smart phone would have been more difficult. There was a distinct lack of smart phones on secondworld. The technology existed equivalent to, and even exceeding world-one, but the motivation to have this widely distributed amongst the populous was no longer there. The financial gain was not to be had, not on a large scale at least. The drive to facilitate and perpetuate the dulling and numbing of society, the control of the masses, was no longer viable. Pockets existed, different methods of controls were in place, but the control en masse, the stranglehold, was no longer so overt.

Mobile phones were available, and residents could apply to the Bureau for one. The process was a bit drawn out so by the time their mobile phone had arrived, they had got used to a life where they were not always

contactable. These were not smart phones. They could make and receive calls, and send and receive messages. That was it. Not even snake.
And each phone issued had the transcription 'This phone is for your convenience, not theirs'.

Every resident had a landline and if you wanted to access the internet this was still available in public libraries. The internet was still a vast and well maintained medium, but with vastly fewer lies. Banal content was also reduced. There were not many that wanted to post pictures of their lunch. This would involve some serious foresight, dedication, and lack of imagination.

As such, a completely phoneless Michael stepped out into the world.

The front door opened out into a cobbled street. When Michael had arrived at the flat it was dark, and he was tired. He had neither the lighting nor the resolve to fully appreciate the beauty of this place. The village was now bustling with activity, more so down at the far end. Michael decided to walk towards the crowds. As he went, he was greeted with either a smile or a 'good morning'. The greetings appeared warm and genuine.

The building he left seemed late Victorian, though probably weren't called that he guessed, as at the time of their construction Queen Victoria would have still been on world-one. Across the road from him sat some more modern dwellings but mixed in with cottages. He discovered the road was named Station Road but was yet to discover any signs of a railway. 'Did they even have railways here?' he thought to himself.

A stone wall ran adjacent to the footpath that he followed. He could see that the gardens were well maintained, and that Cornflower and Sweet Peas were still apparent and would have been in full bloom some months prior. There was a pride to the floristry that would have been prominent in the vast majority of well-maintained villages in world-one, but with the addition of a stronghold of productive planting. Beanpoles shot up at regular intervals, greenhouses and poly-tunnels were prevalent. The front garden of each residence was teeming with vegetation of one type or another. Flowering plants adorning hanging baskets; sunken beds rich with crops. This was similar to the arrangement he had witnessed at the Processing Hub. This industrial enterprise held its own beauty.

He continued West towards the village centre and on to the High Street. The throng of people gathered were partaking in a variety of activities. There was music, dancing, people drinking, people making trade. The smell of something sweet and unhealthy lingered in the air. A brief pang of hunger prompted Michael until he realised he had just eaten. He was also unsure of the arrangements here and doubted he would be able to make a successful transaction for the hot goods. There were market stalls everywhere Michael looked, colonising the streets surrounding the village hall. There were tattoo parlours, he had counted three so far; restaurants and eateries. There was also a pub, The Garden Hermit, which looked particularly lively. This was more than a gathering to make trade; it was a social event.

A church dominated the village centre, the crooked spire pointing to the heavens with the vigour of a sheepish schoolboy raising his hand to be excused. The church, with its replicated medieval architecture, was surrounded by a graveyard. Michael thought for a moment what it must feel like to have known someone buried in the world-one equivalent. To come here only to find a loved one's grave now occupied by a stranger.

The roads were inhabited by people. This in itself was not odd; roads were often closed to vehicles for events such as this, but Michael could not hear the familiar hum of traffic in the distance. The absence of noise only became apparent to him when he went searching for it. As if on cue the sound of horse hoofs erupted and a horse and trap that was previously out of view presented itself in the square. The crowds casually parted and rejoined to allow its travel.

Michael also viewed things that he could not quite fathom. On the main road, as the corner swept around, there was netting standing about 10 feet high. The netting was held up by a metal frame and set at a 45-degree angle.

As he pondered the conundrum a drink was thrust into his hand and the culprit disappeared before Michael had time to protest. It was a cloudy orange colour and it smelt potent with alcohol. A woman walked past wearing a velvet top hat, she was walking a fox on a lead.

Whilst drinking his orange wine Michael turned his attention to one of the houses that had been completely adorned with the brightest and most colourful murals. Flowers, the sea, a dragon. He was unsure how long he spent exploring these works, but it was a joy. He filled his senses – after all he was starting with a clean pallet.

Someone with a penchant for topiary had recreated mount Rushmore.

Everything looked as sturdy as it needed to be. It was all well maintained. There was a practicality about the place, but also a pride. This place looked as if it could stand for a thousand years, but there was also a vibrancy, a passion for life to not only be lived but to be shared. A community without the façade of reverence.

This felt safe, it felt warm.

He could not remember ever visiting Nesfield-upon-Hean on earth-one, but thought it was ideal. The architecture, the cobbled streets, the village green, the lush trees. He saw no reason to apply for a transfer and thought he could be quite happy here, at least until he had figured out what he wanted to do with his remaining 23 years. He would of course want to visit his old neighbourhood to see what changes had been made. No, that was wrong. No changes had been made; this was an entirely different place. It would be more correct to ask what had not been replicated. He knew he would not be able to live in his old house, as he was currently by himself. Again, this did not cause Michael any anxiety whatsoever. He did not hold any attachment to property. He told himself that this was a noble quality.

There was somewhat of a Dickensian feel to the village; perhaps it was the absence of modern trappings or maybe the prevalence of the characters that occupied the square. The majority of people either made their own clothes or adapted the standard issue clothing. The mass-produced generational uniforms were no longer available from the high-street chains, so people improvised, people became more daring, people developed their own style.

As Michael observed the village folk he spotted a scruffy man with a peddle bike. Michael gave the man a glance that was initially cursory. The bike was laden with all sorts of items; a fishing rod, what looked like an epee, a kettle, a set of makeshift panniers either side of the rear wheel, and something else balancing on the frame. As he got closer Michael could see that it was some sort of bird. The man appeared to have a peregrine falcon sitting atop the frame of his bike. It was wearing a hood that covered its eyes, but the bird did not seem to be tethered in any way to the bike frame and seemed content to be pushed along.

What was more, the bird appeared to have some form of shelter further back on the frame, where supposedly the falcon could make use of during wet weather. The man himself was a tall lithe character with a broad grin. He wore a long overcoat with a hooded top underneath, despite the warm weather. His hair was pulled back from his face into a plaited ponytail that ran halfway down his back, his beard was styled into a French Fork. He sported a fingerless glove on one hand, betraying yellow stained fingers, and on the other hand a gauntlet of tan leather.

Michael's inspection of the man was broken as a woman with a red cloak and red hair walked up to him and pushed a leaflet into his hand. She was stunning. Michael thought he might feel more intimidated if he was 'that way inclined' but was still able to admit that he was in absolute awe of her beauty. "The Final Realm is waiting. Come; join us!" she exclaimed. The lady held his gaze for a moment that sat on the cusp of awkwardness before disappearing back into the crowd.

Michael looked down at the leaflet. It read 'The Church of the Holy Extrapolites. Come, rejoice, repent. Embrace the word. Seek the Final Realm.' It reminded him that he had not touched the leaflet he was given yesterday by the Midwife.

"Bin it." a figure said as Michael was gathering his thoughts. Michael looked about himself to confirm that the stranger with the falcon was addressing him. "Bin it." he repeated and pointed towards the leaflet Michael had just been handed. "The Extrapolites," the man continued, "have nothing to do with 'em."

"These people?" Michael held up his leaflet.

"Charlatans, the lot of 'em!" he exclaimed. "They get you to kill yourself, but not until they get anything they can from you."

"I thought people didn't own things?" Michael queried.

"Oh, ownership always seeps in, one way or another." The man propped his bike against the wall and put his hands on his hips. Unperturbed, the falcon kept its post. "They believe that you must pass on before you're allotted 23 years are up. Something to do with a 5th Realm, or something. Least, they say they believe that. The ones who join might, but the ones at the top 'aint believers, just grifters. Charlatans! A suicide club is what it is. Nobody stops them. Who are we to say that there is not another world after this one? Evidence for the existence of life after death is concrete. Still up for debate is whether there is life after seconddeath. Who knows? They do pick some interesting ways to go, I will give them that."

The man was referring to the more commercial side of Extapolite sect. For a fitting donation a secondworlder could choose their method of demise. Skydive without parachute; bungee jump without bungee; catapult. They had even constructed the euthanasia rollercoaster- first-world design, secondworld built. A convert could be sent to the other side by a catapult in Sri Lanka. Far flung destinations, where they could be flung far. Nothing that could be deemed to be cruel. Nothing torturous. No drowning. There were safety regulations to ensure that death was more Mach than macabre. As with everything there were unregulated events that fell outside the scope of good taste, but what real power did anyone have in regulating a group intent on killing themselves.

He put his right hand underneath his left armpit before removing his hand from the gauntlet and extending it to Michael. "I'm Victor. You're new." It wasn't a question. Victor new everyone around here, but also this man had the look of someone green to the secondworld.

-

Once safely back in his flat Michael put the kettle on the stove. He wanted some time to himself. He had agreed to meet the man Victor for a drink the next evening, but for now he would be his own company. He and Victor had got chatting and the man ended up showing Michael around some more of the village. Victor had pushed his falcon laden bike around, pointing out items of interest and answering any questions Michael had. Michael asked him about the netting he had seen earlier. "That's to catch the bodies." Victor explained. "On world-one that corner is a black-spot. You get people taking the bend too fast and crashing their car. Not many die on impact, but enough for them to put up some netting." Michael's confused face betrayed a thousand questions on his lips, so Victor continued. "Imagine it; you crash and go flying through the windscreen, you're killed buy the impact of that, then find yourself flying through the air naked only to crash into a cottage or something. Nets. Needed to happen."

This local knowledge was peppered with titbits about secondworld in general. "Elvis never did turn up on this side you know. I suppose he must have done at some point but when was that? Your guess is as good as mine." Tales of Picasso and Matisse reunited. Teddy Roosevelt's boxing career. Bertrant Russell's annoyance at being alive again; 'he just wanted to rest'.

Michael found the man interesting. Charming even. Michael was not much of a drinker, but neither was he a pioneer and so when the invitation had come to meet Victor in the 'Garden Hermit' he accepted. But now Michael needed to rest. He would have a cup of tea, watch something on the boob-tube and relax for a while.

Declan Treanor

Boob-tube

There was a choice of three terrestrial channels. An unmanned scrolling news channel which seemed to be mainly reporting on the weather, a sports channel and a history channel. The rest of the content was available through streaming.

Sport looked a bit different now, lots of senior players with renewed vigour. Some of those that missed their chance the first time around were able to revisit childhood dreams in leagues and tournaments with an older population. The stadiums, grounds and courts were available. They, like all structures, were replicated to mimic world-one but they were no longer corporate money-making machines, the distraction for the masses, they were simply there to be enjoyed. This was sport in its purest form. Competition for competition's sake. Sunday league at St James'; touch rugby at Twickenham. At this moment it was televising the over 100's tennis.

He switched to the streaming content that he had explored earlier, as he thought the history channel might be a bit heavy and he wanted to switch off.

As he waded through the seemingly endless options a few popped out at him. 'Die Hard' with John Wayne as John McClane. Yippee-Ki-Yay pilgrim!

'Don Quixote' directed by Orson Welles; the TV series 'Manimal' with Howard Hughes for some unknown reason, and B movie, after B movie, after B movie. Michael suspected that anyone was allowed to upload to the platform.

He scrolled through the films, programmes and documentaries for what seemed like an age. Unable to make a decision he turned on the history channel. A documentary on World War II was part way through.

On the secondworld battlefields of World War II humanity was reborn. The first thing the fallen soldiers noticed was the absence of noise. Where was the gunfire, the shelling, the screams? They roused themselves to find that those that had gone before, were waiting with blankets and words of comfort. Again, they had returned to men; not the faceless pawns of power-hungry leaders; not the frontline fodder sacrificed for the greater good. The diktat of the dictators and despots sending young men to their deaths in their millions.

From a secondworld perspective open fields would suddenly become littered with naked and confused men, who moments earlier were part of some campaign or other. The completeness of their vulnerability. Their disorientation, their reliance, at the mercy of those that found them. But they too would become the sate of the masses. They had become tired of war many years before their death. They too would cleanse the battlefield of its torment. "It's over, you can rest now." These words were learned in a variety of languages and repeated throughout from each site of war.

When the concentration camps were discovered all the atrocities that had gone before paled. The anger and outrage that was felt was redirected, and concerted efforts were made to ensure that these places became beacons of love and hope. Structures were created to mimic the world-one buildings, but these were very different. They were crafted from the finest materials and to resemble the architecture of temples and cathedrals. They were painted the brightest of colours and decorated with such love and care. The surrounding areas were adorned with wildflowers. War crimes would be dealt with in good time. This was a place of peace, a place of joy. From fear to respite. The children were welcomed with toys, and games and laughter. Clothes of the finest materials. Their bodies and minds repaired and restored. Skeletal frames now held muscle. The dark rings around eyes were gone. There was food, and drink, and soft but joyful music. Tears were wept. Tears of joy and restoration.

Whole communities were established in those areas and people dedicated themselves to ensuring that within those first moments of passing, those prisoners, now free, would be welcomed in love and hope and harmony.

After the second world war there was a concerted effort to drive a common cause. This was built off the back of those that had sacrificed their lives on the battlefield. These were people who had no thirst for war. They needed to hold those in power to account, and needed to see war crimes atoned for, but they had no desire to return to that field of war. They needed not to rebuild the structures damaged in the war, so they set about rebuilding the society.

Free food, free clothing, free lodgings. 'Let no man want' was the banner of the new world.

Not to say that secondworld was some kind of utopia. People are people. They are self-serving, envious, bitter, and small minded. People take things the wrong way, they take offence, they take things that don't belong to them, they take. People carve out their own self-worth through the destruction of others and leave the shells of those poor creatures discarded in the path of our societal construct. Not caring if they are trampled underfoot of the masses. Not caring if they are unable to contain the burden of their being. Not giving a second thought to their fodder, or worse, relishing in the misery they have borne.

But with trauma resolved, a finite timeframe for existence and a world built by the oppressed, on secondworld the human race stood the best chance they ever had to pull themselves out of the gutter.

Adolf Hitler, as you would imagine, spent his time incarcerated until his execution. This took some time whilst proper renumeration was sought. His execution was delayed not through some misguided empathy, it was to ensure that as many of his victims could have their day in court. Day after day, each gave testimony of their suffering.

The Fuhrer was made to sit through this testimony. The trial ran daily for a total of one thousand, eight hundred and twenty-six days, commencing on the 8th May 1945. Each and every day, no respite. Jurors and Judges were on rotation, each retired intermittently, passing their verdict before they retired. The likes of which had not been seen, with a hope that it would not be seen again. Hitler had a dedicated security team around him. This was more to prevent suicide than homicide. Though it was true that the masses wanted to see him hang, they also knew the importance and significance of the trial. The atrocities were detailed and documented. This was reparation, healing on a global scale, but it was also tempered with stoicism; it needed to be, to show the distinction between good and evil. Each day the atrocities that he had designed were laid out before him, and each evening he would be visited by a religious cleric to hear his confession.

When the date for his execution was finally set, official envoys whose 23 years fell before the date, agreed to take forward the message that he was coming should there be a world-three.

Hitler was hanged to death on 29th April 1969.

Michael sat for a while absorbing all that he had learned. He ate a simple meal in silence and retired to bed.

Declan Treanor

Dirt Sticks to Sweat

Jackie Taylor used to have a 50cm scar running from the base of her calf to the upper part of her thigh. Since being reborn this had vanished. As with the majority of the populace she came to accept this. It was only years later when she got particularly muddy dancing in a field, along with about 10,000 other revellers, she discovered that the scar had not totally gone. Whilst her legs had become, for the most part, evenly dusted in dirt, an outline of clean skin could be found where her scar used to be. She asked around following this discovery. She was informed, when recounting the story, by an ex-surgeon, that deep wounds didn't regenerate sweat glands, and dirt sticks to sweat. This was likely the reason for the patches.

It seemed strange to her, and to others, that her scar tissue would be repaired but not her sweat glands. Some people grew back whole arms, parts of their brain. The more she thought of it, people who had been decapitated had come to secondworld with their heads firmly on their shoulders.

It bothered her to the extent of a talking point. She wished nobody who had grown back a head ill-will, and the fact that she was missing some sweat glands in her leg mattered nought to her. She just thought it yet another curiosity of this world. An oddity, that was only remarkable in caparison. She was also missing a tattoo she had been quite fond of but had not yet bothered to replace it.

Jackie once met a man with stars in his eyes. This was not a euphemism; he had literal star patterns embedded in his eyes. His name was Tern. He was kind and gentle, though Jackie had the suspicion that in his previous life he had been less kind and less gentle.

He had first-died though electrocution.

Jackie later found out that it was common, people who died through electrocution usually had stars in their eyes, but at the time it had been a thing of beauty.

People who had lost parts of themselves often found them in place again. Toes and fingers, arms and legs. Not just those lost at the time of their death, limbs that had been lost decades prior. It came as quite a shock to some. Poor eyesight was now 20/20, and more regularly than not, blindness was cured. Piercings had repaired themselves and tattoos had gone. People of secondworld were not born into the wrong gendered body.

There were some anomalies though. Sometimes a missing leg would not reappear and there didn't seem to be a logic to it, whereas there were no documented cases where a decapitation was not recapitated.

The plastic surgeons' knife did not follow you to secondworld. For some, that had been systematically butchered over decades, this was a rebirth. They were able to see themselves again. Able to love themselves again. With their trauma missing, this was easier.

Apart from the scar Jackie's appearance in secondworld had changed little, at least not in her minds-eye. On world-one Jackie was a police officer, and when she wasn't at work she was at the gym. She was physically fit bordering on being muscular. Her abdominal muscles were her pride and the line that contoured her thigh muscles were her joy. This was not shallow vanity; this was satisfaction of a job well done. This was about obtaining peak physically fitness.

But life had other plans for Jackie.

After the cancer had finished with her, she was nothing but skin and bone. Day-by-day she watched herself become less, watched herself ebb away. Each day finding it harder to do the things she took for granted. It became harder to run, harder to walk, harder to eat, harder to breathe, harder to live.

When she was reborn, she became herself again.

She was overjoyed to have herself back. Her old self. The self that she always pictured herself to be, even at her weakest.

Jackie decided to join the police force again. She asked around and ended up at the door of a man named Innocent. "So, you want to be our police."

Jackie was to learn she would be a 'force of one.' That was okay. As it turned out there was not much crime. It was mainly disputes and misdemeanours, or lost dogs. It was difficult to admit that the lack of crime bothered her, but it did. There were some crimes of course. 'Criminals gonna criminal.' She always said but if you have your immediate needs met, your trauma gone, and a society that does not value excessive wealth, then it's less likely.

It was early morning. Jackie left the house. She would need to pick up some more heroin on her way home, she was running low.

-

The war on drugs was over. There was no war. People could grow their own or produce their own. They could trade or produce as a community, but there were not the profits to be made as before. No drug lords, no need to criminalise the user. The reasons for drug use had changed. People were not trying to block out trauma, and generally they were not attempting to escape their circumstances. Most of all there was lots of help and support for those that needed it.

Scientists, doctors, architects, nutritionists, physicists were the new leaders. Those that knew something about the field advised. Experts provided their expertise.

Gone was the traditional role of the politician. It was not needed in this world. The more society evolved, the harder it became to articulate the reason why this role would be needed, not only in this world, but in any functioning system.

It became more and more apparent that the role of a politician was to ensure that the role of the politician existed. Once the grift was recognised, it could not be unseen. Or was this too a façade? A veneer of civility. There were the Bureau's, of course, but these provided more of an admin role. A link between the various communities and the Thinktanks. And the Thinktanks were headed by people who thought.

The 'Rat Park' experiments by Bruce K. Alexander had been conducted in the 1970's on world-one. His findings indicated there was need for drastic change on how western governments addressed addiction, but it seemed there was more to gain by continuing the status quo than listening to those who knew what they were talking about. The experiment involved giving the rats a choice between drugged or undrugged water. Put simply, if the rats were entertained with toys, activities and social interaction they were less likely to self-administer. When starved of stimulus they overdosed. Though this research was cited and actioned at a local level, in the main world-one governments either ignored this, or worst still used it to destroy whole communities.

Stigmatisation was never the answer. On this world the efforts that had previously went into fighting and shaming drug use, were redirected to ensuring that these people were part of the community. The addict disappeared. There were times when people used more than they should, but on the whole, they were supported. The shunning was replaced with warmth and acceptance.

Jackie was a user. She had not been on world-one but needed something now, something that her job had previously provided. It was not an issue. Not as yet.

Catney

Michael felt rested after his sleep. He would spend the day exploring the local area but would not go too far. He had a feeling that the evening yet to come with the falcon man, may prove to be hard work. Michael had some fruit for breakfast and packed some provisions in a small bag for his lunch. He put the three table coins in his pocket, just in case, and left the flat. If at all possible, he would avoid spending these; he would need them later.

Michael left the boundary of Nesfield-upon-Hean and walked toward the neighbouring village of Catney. It was mild and he thought the stroll would be pleasurable. He also wanted to see what Catney had to offer. He crossed over the hump-back bridge that marked the transition from town to country, letting the signposts direct the way.

Michael noticed that the roads here, as in the village, were constructed of typical road building materials, that was to say that there were cobbled streets and tarmacked roads. This in isolation was not strange, it was only strange by comparison. The thought was only just occurring to him that when he came to on the motorway, the road surface was very different. It was sponge-like, pliable, but still firm enough for the midwives' truck to drive on. This, he supposed, made perfect sense. Crashes on motorways were more likely to be at speed. A soft landing would be welcome.

He continued his journey.

Lush green grazing fields sat aside fields of barley and wheat. Wind turbines, in a variety of shapes and sizes, dotted the landscape at regular intervals. In some of the fields he could see tarpaulin stretched out. Michael guessed correctly that it was for the collection of water.

In the Kingdom you had your daily allowance of water. The allowance was adequate and ensured that there was ample for all, without wastage. Your shower water became your bathwater your bathwater became the water for the plants. If you wanted more you could source it, there was nothing wrong with that as long as it was not to the detriment of others. Set up a water butt; ask a neighbour who was not using all theirs; go down to the river. If you needed some additional for some project or another, you stretched out a tarpaulin.

As he neared Catney a horse and trap went past at moderate speed. The driver tipped her bowler hat to Michael as she passed. This was the first person he had seen since leaving Nesfield-upon-Hean and it was almost as if Michael had forgotten about the existence of other humans. On approach to Catney he began to recognise other signs of life. He heard the bustle of activity, chatter and the calling out from market traders. There were always market traders it seemed.

Basic needs—food, clothing, shelter—were freely provided, liberating individuals from the shackles of survival, but trade was always present. You want some wool? I want some wine. You have some fish? I have some corn.

People also traded their time. I'll teach you to play the piano if you teach me to paint.

Hobbies, once pushed to the sidelines, experienced a renaissance.

In this societal evolution, the pursuit of a fulfilling life took precedence over the relentless chase after financial success. The air was filled with a sense of contentment, as individuals embraced a new paradigm that allowed them to live, work, and find meaning at a pace that resonated with the rhythm of their own lives.

The pace of life slowed.

Michael walked through Catney, happy to be there for no particular reason other than to be there.

A man walking in the opposite direction stopped in front of Michael. The man's name was Francis. "Hi, I'm Francis." Francis said. "Pleased to meet you." said Michael. He shook the man's hand and the man continued on his way. Michael never met Francis again. Ever.

In some ways it was very much a quintessentially British village. World-one British, secondworld Kingdomish. The buildings were similar to those in Nesfield-upon-Hean, a composite picture of old and new, but with the addition of a monorail system running overhead. He could see that the stanchions for the monorail had been carefully built into the fabric of the village, incorporating pre-existing structures. He imagined that the monorail serviced areas far-afield but was unable to confirm this from his current viewpoint.

Michael came across an unoccupied bench and thought this might be the ideal place to enjoy his lunch. His journey had triggered his appetite. He sat himself down and put his knapsack on his lap. He retrieved the small parcel of food and his water bottle.

It was difficult, he thought, to sit on a bench without an accessory. You needed a coffee, or a sandwich, or a book, or an obedient dog. Just sitting, without anything would be considered odd. Or maybe it wouldn't in this new world. Maybe people could just be themselves, without judgement, without having to justify their existence. To just exist. And to exist imperfectly. To be odd without excuse.

He unwrapped the bread, cheese, and cold meat. Michael had not formed this into a sandwich, instead taking bites out of each in turn. At the time of preparation Michael had thought to himself that he may like to try his meal this way. He was unsure why. Thoughts of Parisian workmen came to the fore. He was right, he did like eating like this but still had no idea why.

He watched the people, but they watched him too. Eye contact was the norm in secondworld, not just the dalliance of scoundrels, or the exchange of lovers.

Michael glugged at his water, then tore in the bread with his teeth. Before swallowing the bread he took a bite of the cheese and then the meat. He chewed for some time before washing it down with another swig of water.

Across the way there was a tall man. He was in the process of taking a series of curved panels from a trolley and was attempting to balance them upright whilst fitting them together. Just as Michael thought that he would cut short his lunch and go and help the man, a second man, as old as dust, had appeared and proceeded to lend a hand. They both juggled and jostled the curved metal sheets into position. Michael wondered what the contraption was. It would have been easy to approach the two men and enquire, and he was sure that they would be more than willing to explain the device, but there was something about the mystery that Michael enjoyed. He hoped he would be able to talk about this spectacle to others, with them being as perplexed as he, proffering best guesses and shots in the dark. A 'Rube Goldberg' machine? Perhaps, but to what end?

A child walked past the scene with its mother. His eyes were naturally drawn to the moving objects that interrupted his vista. He followed their pace with his eyes and then returned his gaze to the scene. Michael's brow furrowed. There was something wrong, but he could not quite see it. Then it hit him. That was the first child he had seen since arriving here. He returned his attention to the boy and woman. Was she his mother? Perhaps not. He looked away, suddenly conscious that the child may experience a lot of eyes on them, given that they were, thankfully, a rarity in this world.

The tall man and the man as old as dust had completed their task and had bid each other good day. It was still unclear to Michael what the purpose of the contraption was.

The joy of his deconstructed sandwich had waned, but he had no regrets about his experiment. It had been fun while it lasted. Michael ripped open the bread and pushed and squished the remaining meat and cheese into it. He took a large bite and another glug from his water bottle.

Michael was just contemplating the journey home when an almighty clamp broke the din of the crowds. He heard it before he saw it. A roar. He feared that something was collapsing and looked about himself. The roar was so alien yet so familiar. A split second after his brain made sense of the sound an AC Cobra presented itself from the far side of the main street.

It was an oddity in secondworld and the crowds waved and whooped as it passed. It was silver with two navy blue stripes running across the bonnet, down the centre of its body. It had obviously been lovingly recreated and as it approached the illusion of similarity dissolved. Tin cans and painted drainpipes had played a part in its construction. It was still a thing of beauty. A work of art. And a valid form of transport.

Declan Treanor

The more he saw of secondworld the more Michael thought that he would enjoy exploring this world and being part of this world.

He needed to get back to rest before drinks with Victor. He might have a look at that Welcome Book when he got home. Maybe find out a few more things.

4.54 billion years

Michael found himself at the kettle again. He could never have imagined that the afterlife would revolve around tea as much as it did. He packed the loose-leaf tea into the infuser and dropped it into the mug, hooking the delicate chain to the outside rim. He poured on the water and left the tea to brew while he turned his attention to the Welcome Book.

He scanned the contents page.

Some had mysterious headings, such as 'The Death of Hopscotch'. Other headings were far more mundane; 'How to apply for free food'; 'COVID'; 'Monorail timetable'; 'Your daily tea allowance'. He mentally bookmarked the last section for later.

He settled on 'Science and nature' which had two sides of A4 dedicated to the subject. Quite succinct, he thought, for the entirety of science and nature.

The best scientific minds of world-one managed to cram in another 23-years of research and experimentation and in addition to new innovation, whatever could be measured was measured.

As far as could be established secondworld was formed about 4.54 billion years ago. It turned on its own axis every 23 hours, 56 minutes and 4 seconds. The circumference of secondworld about 24,898 miles and spun at about 1,037 mph. The Moon rotated at the same rate that it revolved around secondworld and was an average of 238,855 miles away. The secondworld Sun was established to be approximately 93 million miles away or roughly 8.20 light minutes. The speed of light stood at 299,792,458 metres per second.

Mercury followed the Sun, Venus followed Mercury, and secondworld after that. Mars, Jupiter, Saturn, Uranus, and Neptune presented themselves as they had done in the space that held world-one.

There was nothing measurable by science that could distinguish between the physics of the two worlds.

Some evolutionary aspects differed, but these could be explained. Outside of this there were two outright anomalies. There were no platypuses on secondworld; and most penguins were now yellow and white.

This did not stop the continued quest for irregularities by the scientific community.

Michael thought to himself that he could have guessed this information. Not about the penguins or the platypuses, but the other stuff, sure. It was nice to have it confirmed though.

Drinking with Victor

It was late into the evening, but the night sky still maintained its brightness. The lanterns that lined the streets were not required but were still welcomed. They added yet more beauty to the already picturesque scene. The air was warm. As Michael made his way through the cobbled streets, he was greeted by those that passed. Some nodded their head in acknowledgement, some offered a 'good evening' or 'lovely night', there was even a tip of the hat from a dapper older gentleman. Michael could hear the pub before he saw it. And as he opened the door, he could distinctly make out Victor who was mid rant. "Some people think they have a right to an exalted position. Bemoaning the removal of their privilege. They gasp. They choke. 'Why am I no longer able to spit in the eye of those born out of favour. It is unfair that I should have the same footing as the hoi polloi. It is my God given right to have rights above the meagre. The meek shall not inherit this earth.' Clawing at the possessions of others. A pox to these people, I say! A pox."

As is customary in village pubs, when the door opened all eyes went to it. "Michael!" Victor bellowed. "Everyone! Everyone! This is my good friend Michael." Victor announced, "He is a sinner…but aren't we all." A good-natured cheer rose up from the attending mob. "Michael, what is your poison?" Michael edged his way through the crowds to his new friend and shook his hand.

"I'll just get my own," said Michael "I've only got the three coins from the flat."

"Not likely!" Came the reply. "I invited you for a drink, and that is what we shall have. Put your money away. So, Michael, what is your poison?"

"Whatever's good." Michael gambled.

"Two brandies barkeep, if you will." Said Victor turning to the bar. "I will sub you today for there will be work tomorrow!" Victor said loudly and then muttered in Michael's ear "Not literally tomorrow, you understand? It's a phrase. You can pay me back another time; or do me a favour some time; or never pay me back. I don't mind."

On receiving the brandies Victor handed one to Michael raised his own "Claret is the liquor for the boys; port for men; but he who aspires to be a hero must drink brandy." He clinked glasses with Michael's. "Dr Johnson." He took a sip whilst keeping eye contact with Michael; he considered this the correct way to conduct a toast. "They say he had Tourette's syndrome."

"Who? Dr Johnson?" Michael asked, not really being absolutely sure who Dr Johnson was, but not willing to admit that just yet.

"Yeah. Posthumously, of course. There was no such thing back then." Victor took another sip. "Double posthumously I suppose."

Michael had already become accustomed to Victor's speeches. He liked them. He liked him, he liked being around him, and others did too. He did not see the man pay for a drink all night. Victor, when not soapboxing to the gathered patrons, was regaling Michael with the history and politics of secondworld. This inevitably led to more soapboxing and the cycle continued.

"Why would you allow one person to have all the money?" Some of Victor's favourite pastimes were drinking brandy and lambasting the capitalist structures of world-one. "It just doesn't make sense. 'But they worked hard to get there.'" Victor continued in a mocking tone. "You wanna tell me that Elon Musk has worked 248 billon times harder than I have in his lifetime?" Victor had worked out these figures in a not-so-scientific manner but had memorised them and loved to quote them as it illustrated his point well. He continued "So, is it every day that he gets up and works 248 billon times more than everyone else, or does he work 347.2 billion times harder than everyone else on weekdays and has weekends off?" By and large Victor was guilty of preaching to the converted.

The movement away from a capitalist structure on secondworld was somewhat dictated by circumstance. You arrived on with nothing. You only had 23 years. Was this enough time to build an empire? Any power or influence was lost. Your family before you arrived with nothing. What could they have built up in 23 years? What could be hidden or squirreled away? You also had no guarantee that your offspring would reach secondworld before your demise. You could not sire more. Nobody new was born on secondworld, it was populated purely by the dead of world-one.

And what was your motivation to try to scrabble your dynasty back? Why waste your 23?

Some adjusted better than others. Those who wielded vast power in world-one were most likely to struggle with the new structure, and the redressing of wealth and power in secondworld. Some on arrival attempted to claw back some control. From time-to-time alliances were formed, plots were plotted, and coups were attempted, but nothing stuck. The masses were in no hurry to be corralled back into their submissive roles. Momentum for a return to type could not be gained, no matter how hard the ex-elite rocked the boat in an attempt to capsize it.

People were just living their lives. The usual thumbscrews were not relevant. They no longer applied to society. There was no grift to be grifted. People were fed, people had shelter, people had a chance to be reborn, to revisit themselves and how they chose to exist. How they chose to see out those 23-years they had been gifted. A chance to make those 23-years count for something. And when the riches and glory were no longer tied to what they desired, their desires changed. People had new experiences, travelled and explored, but for the vast majority they found meaning in creating a community, a place to welcome others, and to live out their days in peace and harmony.

A lot of roles were now automated, not to save a penny but to save a back. People were still needed in a variety of roles, but nobody needed to work themselves into early graves. Food, clothing, shelter, all free; but if you wanted to travel, buy some treat food, buy a guitar, you needed to find a bit of work. Some people worked just for items. Some picked up a job and realised they liked it. When the emphasis moved from new car, new kitchen, new house, and money, and money, and money; people found they could relax into themselves. People found hobbies again. People whittled. Victor whittled. But at this moment he ranted.

"World-one is doomed. Gone are the bar room philosophers. It is unacceptable to devote any time to contemplation. 'What did you do last night?' 'I thought about my existence, where I am in the universe and where I am in relation to the universe. I thought about time. The construct of time. The marching of it, and my mortality. I thought about not existing in a conscious state. I thought about the universe with me, and without man. I thought about a universe returning to a singularity.' This is not a socially acceptable pastime. If this is your job, then this is somehow fine. You would be better to state that you spent your time watching old episodes of 'Boat Island' or some such fodder. This is a life lived. This is the expected behaviour. But no more. Not here. But what good is that, if world-one is destroyed? They take us with them on their march to oblivion." Victor was rambling now. Michael didn't mind. There was something enjoyable about it. Something soothing. Not the topics, the topics were often horrific, but there was some poetry in the despair.

"Capitalism is set up for reprobates. If you steal something here, what are you going to do with it? Use it yourself? Fine. You've got it now, no need to steal it again. You have food, water, clothing, shelter. You don't need to steal for that. You want drugs, then grow some. You want a fast car? There are none. Are you stealing for profit? What is profit? I'll tell you what profit is, it's more than you need."

"Come on Vic," the landlord interjected when he thought it safe to do so "why don't we have a song instead?"

Victor raised his glass to communicate abdication from the floor. Up until now Michael had assumed the instruments that adorned the walls were purely ornamental but when the call came for song these instruments were passed around the group, and tuning commenced.

"Do you play?" Michael was asked by one of the group; a short, stocky man with big hands and a broad smile.

"No. I've always wanted to but never got around to it." He answered.

"Then today is the day my friend, today is the day." Said the man who then proceeded to place some kind of stringed instrument in Michael's lap and manipulate his arms to what he deemed to be the correct position.

Michael's protestations were met with "Carpe Diem, my lad, Carpe Diem!"

Victor led Michael to the edge of the village to where the canal bridge sat. They took the sloped pathway towards the towpath. It was dark with the men reliant on the moonlight to guide them, but Victor was well versed in staggering back home in the pitch black and led the way with confidence. From time-to-time he would warn Michael of unseen obstacles. "Make sure to duck under the branch here." or "Watch your step on this next bit, there's a big dip." They made their way from the canal walkway into the adjoining field, then into the woodlands. On entering the woodland, they obviously had the additional obstacle of the trees to contend with, but the ground evened out and was surprisingly level.

Michael had just begun the mental composition of a sentence to ask how far away the hut was. He was trying his best to construct it in a way that did not make him sound like a child on a family holiday. He was not having much success but all of a sudden, the point became moot. They came into a clearing bathed in moonlight with a wooden hut framed by the surrounding trees.

The structure was modest yet inviting, nestled amongst the brothers of its construction. The roof, slightly pitched to allow rainwater to run off, was made of wooden shingles that had weathered over time, adding to the hut's quaint and homely feel.

Extending from the front of the hut was a porch, elevated slightly above the ground. The porch was supported by robust wooden posts, each one unique with its own knots and imperfections, giving it character. A simple wooden railing ran around the perimeter, offering a sense of safety without obstructing the view of the forest beyond. The floor of the porch was made of wide wooden planks, worn smooth from years of use, with a few creaky spots that told stories of countless footsteps.

A rocking chair sat on the porch; its seat slightly curved for comfort. The door to the hut was solid and inviting, with a simple brass handle and a brace of pheasants hung to the left of the frame. Flanking the door were a couple of windows with wooden shutters, which could be closed during storms or at night. Victor had designed and built the structure himself and was extremely proud of his dwelling. Of course, he would never admit this; but equally would not deny it if challenged.

Its rustic charm blended seamlessly with the natural surroundings. The men entered the cabin.

"I'm gonna have to teach you how to play parcheesi." Said Victor, clumsily making his way through the threshold. He lit a match, then lit an oil lamp which hung to the left of the door opening. Victor unhooked the lamp and placed it on a nest of tables that was flanked by two armchairs.

"Sit, sit." Victor said as he busied himself lighting two more lamps and collecting glasses and a bottle which Michael guessed was more alcohol.

There was a fireplace to the right of the nest of tables, but this had not been used during the summer months. The area of the cabin which could be referred to as a kitchen held a butcher's block table, it looked like this was the area where Victor would prepare meat; a ceramic sink with a cast iron tap that needed to be pumped; a narrow cabinet where Victor had retrieved the glasses and bottle; and a wood burning stove. Neighbouring the kitchen area was an area that was curtained off. Michael guessed this would be the bedroom. Victor separated the nest and proceeded to put the drinks and glasses on one table, moved the lamp to the smallest table and placed the largest table of the three between the two chairs. "Pour the drinks, good man." Victor said as he went to fetch the boardgame.

Michael looked at the bottle. The contents were bright green. Looking around the shack there were various items that hung from the walls. Skillets, a pot, and a waffle iron and various other items of cast iron. An axe, a hatchet, a longbow and a quiver full of arrows. A large tin bath. In between these items wooden posts jutted out at regular intervals. As Michael studied these posts, pondering their use, he suddenly thought of the falcon. It hadn't come home with them and neither had the bicycle. "Where's the bird?" Michael questioned.

"She'll make her own way home." Victor plonked himself in the armchair opposite and began to unpack the game and set up the board and pieces.

"What about the bike? Asked Michael.

"It'll be right." Came the reply. "Now, I said I was gonna teach ya parcheesi without askin if you play."

"I think I've heard of it. Don't think I've ever played it though." Michael conceded.

"Even so, it was wrong of me to presume." Victor admitted "To presume is to make a pre out of you and me."

Michael grinned, took a sip of his drink and winced.

"Oh, I nearly forgot." Said Victor and got up again, gathering some sugar, the matches and an ornate spoon. "It's absinthe!" he declared "We have to treat it with the respect it deserves."

Victor taught Michael parcheesi and how to drink absinthe. They talked way into the early hours. The falcon returned at some point, gaining entry to the cabin through some undisclosed passage. Michael learned the falcon's name that night. He also learned about the man. The man that is and the man that was.

Victor had been an insurance broker from Leeds. He had been visiting area on business when he died and just decided to stay. "You wouldn't have recognised me back then. Short hair, clean shaven. Suit."

He was old when he died, not in years but in body. He felt it. It had crept up on him. He had glimpses of the man to come. He felt more tired on the odd day, harder to put on socks. Some days he felt young and had forgot himself. But the young man became more distant. He forgot how to be joyful, he forgot how to be light, carefree.

"This secondworld was a second chance for me. I never knew life could be like this. This is the person I always should have been." Victor threw the dice and rolled a five and a two. He moved his piece of the board. "I worked, and worked, and worked. And I had this thought that one day I would be content and would have achieved enough to be happy. The next house, then all would be well. The next promotion and I would be able to rest on my laurels. I never had a family. Never had time. It was probably for the best; it wouldn't have changed who I was. I would have worked and worked and thought I was doing the best for them and provided them with everything, but time. Everything but myself."

"Then I came here…The phrase 'you can't take it with you' was right, wasn't it?" Victor moved his piece to the blue square. "I remember my first day here like it was yesterday. Cold, naked, bewildered. But light. Like the albatross had been lifted from around my neck; and I didn't realise the weight of it until it was gone."

"I took on a ward, you know. Yes, I took on a lad." His eyes wet before, now began to stream. He wiped them in turn with the sleeve of the arm which held the hand that held his glass. "He was 6 years old when he came to me. I taught him what it was to be a man, and he taught me what it was to be a good man. Charles was his name; still is. He lives in New Zealand with his beautiful wife and the children they have taken on. The last time he wrote they had five, but they were talking about more." Victor composed himself and the pair held silence, but for the roll of the dice and the click of the pieces on the board. This continued until Victor was ready to resume one of his prepared speeches. A speech that was not divorced from the man but was not a raw open wound.

"Living on borrowed time, we are all living on borrowed time. To the dust we shall return. It was always, and will always be. Long after the conscious us is gone, the matter that made us shall continue to be. Matter changes state but does not cease to exist. Planets will end, suns will burn out and die, but matter is eternal. What was used to create us had always been there, since the beginning of everything. We are the stars."

-

After three games of parcheesi they took their drinks out to the porch. The pitch-black trees that surrounded them were silhouetted against the midnight blue sky. Victor lit up a woodbine. The woodbine had a distinct odour to it.

"It's the young ones that get me. At least 23-years is better than the zero years they had before. There is always the hope of a world-three. There is always hope…Mind your twenty-three, it goes in a dash." Victor wagged his finger in Michael's face; much closer than a sober man would.

"And how long have you got left?" Michael blurted out and immediately regretted the question "Sorry, that's personal. I shouldn't have asked."

"Not at all!" Victor beamed "I've got about five weeks."

"Jesus!" Michael exclaimed. He had no other words.

"It's probably more like four and a half weeks now." Victor continued "What day is it? Wednesday, I reckon? Yeah, four weeks four days. It's not that I don't care about dying but I aint going to be doing a big countdown. I have nothing different planned for my last day. Every day will be my last. I just want to be with friends." Victors smile drifted "Are you my friend Michael?" The question had weight to it. Michael scrambled his words but affirmed that to Victor that he was. The sombre tone immediately left the room and Victor was once again in jovial mood.

"Look at those stars Michael. Look at them." He draped an arm over Michael's shoulder and pointed skyward "They show us how insignificant we are, how futile are our hopes and dreams, how petulant our wishes, at exactly the same time as showing us how majestically beautiful our existence truly is. We are miracles. Pathetic, monstrous miracles." With that, Victor sat down on the ground. His eyes faraway, wistful.

It's not dead

He was sitting on the sofa, a meal on his lap. It was his old house on world-one. There were two sofas in the old lounge, set at right angles to each other, in the shape of an L. Darren was on the other sofa eating his meal. They were watching a programme. It was loud and bright.

"You need to get rid of that." said Darren and gestured with his knife, directing Michael to look at the seat next to him. A cat was outstretched on the seat cushion, splayed belly up. Its throat was slit.

"I will." said Michael and continued with his meal. Michael continued to watch but could no longer hear the television. All he could hear was his mastication of animal flesh and the pulse inside his jugular. The sound intensified, but Michael could not swallow the meat nor slow his heart. The sound grew, becoming increasingly intrusive. Darren was saying something that Michael could not make out. "Sorry, what did you say?" The sounds suddenly abated.
"That thing's not dead." Darren declared. Michael snapped around to see the cat bloody but alive staring at him. Michael woke.

Hangover

When Michael woke for a second time to a drilling sound it took him longer than it should have done to realise that the sound was not external. Michael was not used to hangovers and certainly not hangovers of this magnitude. He smacked his dry mouth. This hurt. He adjusted his body. Each movement brought a new pain.

He was in no condition to go out. He attempted sleep but the throb in his head would not let him.

There was a knock at the door. It took Michael some time to register this. He shuffled to the door, too cognitively impaired to dismiss the notion of answering it. His main focus was to reach the door before they knocked again. The wide grin of Victor greeted him on the other side. "I thought you might need some sustenance." He said in a hushed bellow and held up a brown paper bag in one hand and a glass mason jar in the other. "You sit yourself down and I'll sort us out." Michael complied, throwing himself into the nearest sofa, though the attempt was to gently lower himself. He was aware of the quiet clattering of plates, and the unholy thundering of tin cups being placed softly on the worktop. He closed his eyes for a moment until he was unceremoniously ordered to sit up. A plate was thrust into one hand and a cup in the other. Michael adjusted and balanced the plate on his lap. He was unconvinced of the structural integrity of this manoeuvre. Michael tentatively took a sip from the cup and eyed the plate from above.

A shaky hand gasped hold of the hot sandwich of salty meat. He held it up and manoeuvred it to the general area of his face. He took a bite. His swallow was aided by a more healthy mouthful of the juice.

As the thumping in Michael head abated, he vowed there and then not to touch another drop of alcohol in his life. "This is nice." The first words Michael had uttered since Victor's arrival "What is it?"
"Blueberry Gin." Came the reply.

Florence Ward

Florence Ward had always been a nervous individual; this had previously led her to be overly fastidious in her work and resulted in her becoming quite successful. She was of slight build but physically fit. In secondworld all the anxiety she had previously harboured had disappeared. The crippling desire to please others had gone, and she was calm and relaxed in her own self. However, the years of habit-forming attention to detail and work ethic had remained. She was happiest when she was busy. Florence was currently 97 years old. She would not make 100. This slightly niggled Florence from time to time, it was a number that could be seen as being unfinished. It irked her, but only vaguely, she had cemented to becoming 99. She would not join the Extrapolites, and clock out on 98, though an even number would suit her better.

Florence was English but lived in America for most of her adult life on world-one. She returned to England shortly before her own demise and many years after the death of her husband. There was nobody to keep her in America. No partner, no children, and her friends, one-by-one, had moved from the city. If her Leonard had still been with her, she may well have found herself in some suburb with a white picket fence.

There were would-be suitors, especially in her twilight years, but Florence would pay them no mind. Loud and brash and full of vim. These men would delight in showing her how potent they were. She felt this was a peculiarity of the American male of a certain age. They would perform an extremely brief, and monumentally underwhelming display of acrobatics upon meeting them either before or just following a declaration of their age. "I'm 76 years young!" they would declare, before doing three movements that could, at a push, be generously referred to as 'star jumps'. A set of lunges followed by "Not bad for 73!". All golf trousers, polo-shirts and non-slip loafers.

Her Leonard had been an American. She wondered if he had turned into an acrobatic yank when he was in secondworld. She thought perhaps not, it was more of a world-one phenomenon, and besides she could not picture Leonard doing something like that. That said, she could not imagine Leonard old at all. To her he was forever young. She missed him dearly, and if she had have known about secondworld she would have happily joined him here so they could see out their days together. As it was, he had died young and she had died old and 23 years was not enough to reunite them.

Sketching was popular on secondworld. People adorned their spaces with recreations of photographs of loved ones they had left behind. With no reference other than memory some efforts were more realistic than others, and it may be easy for the individual to become frustrated by the limits of their own talent, but it was the sentiment that prevailed. This was a representation of someone that you had loved and lost.

Florence had attempted to draw her husband. It was a humble, childish effort. A neighbour who was an excellent artist suggested that she draw a picture for her. Florence described him as best she could. When it was completed, Florence thought that it was an excellent picture of someone else. She displayed it in her lounge but never looked at it. It wasn't him. When she wanted to remember Leonard, she looked at her own drawing, the simple childlike drawing that held the essence of him.

When people came to secondworld there was solace in the thought that the lives of their nearest and dearest were continuing elsewhere, but the loss was the same. There was always the chance that you could meet again, not the hope, never the hope, as you would never wish a shortened life upon any of your beloved. The chance that you would meet, but with the knowledge that this may never happen. Some left gifts; this was allowed. Small gifts that gave the ones to follow some insight into how their loved one's lives were lived. How their time was meted out. Letters, pictures, poems. A message across time and place.

Florence had such letters from Leonard but had not yet found the strength to read them.

October

'Morning'. It was a mild October morning, just after 9am. The signs of autumn were just presenting themselves, but only noticeable if you sought them out. It had been a scorching summer and had remained mild up until now. Michael was still wearing shorts, though he would continue this into the winter if occasion allowed. The only hint in his apparel that pointed toward the season, was that he was wearing a slightly thicker hoodie.

Michael liked to wear shorts most of the time, he especially liked to wear them when the weather was a little cooler or when the nights were longer. He liked the thought that others were thinking it was too cold for shorts. This was not the whole reason he liked to wear shorts, but if he were honest, it played a big part in his decision making. He was not the kind to dress informally, when formal attire was required. No. He would not turn up to a wedding or a posh night out dressed inappropriately, but if he could get away with shorts he would.

The rest of him would be wrapped up. He wore hoodies, coats, hats, the whole shebang if required. Michael had used his clothing allowance modestly. He had picked some options that he knew he would wear on a regular basis. He could not think of a current scenario that would require a suit, say, but thought he may pick up a few hours work if this was later required.

'Morning' he replied. Michael was taking a walk along the canal. The Grand Union Canal was the longest canal in the Kingdom. Michael had been informed of this by one of the signs stationed along the route. He assumed that this had also been the case in world-one but was unsure. He had just passed Catney and was walking North. If he turned around and walked South for a few days, this canal would take him to London.

The canal curved its way to the park. At various intervals there were steps or ramps leading to civilisation. Ascending the stairs with no intention of leaving the canal seemed mischievous, but Michael would do this from time-to-time. Popping up out of the canal to spy on those 'terra firmaians' who were oblivious of the subterranean canal community of dog walkers and joggers. All that pass were ready with a morning greeting. A barge captain, tufty and scruffy mirroring his Jack Russell. A lady of advanced years, wearing a straw hat sitting on a bench, throwing grain to the ducks. Canoeists giving an impression of speed against the amblings of the tow path folk, briefly disturbing the carpet of fallen leaves that spread evenly across the water and leaving an undulating corridor in its wake. Red holly berries punctuating the browns and greens. Glimpses of Autumn.

Football teams completed their practice, readying themselves for the Sunday matches. These parks were filled with youth on world-one. These were now replaced by the middle-aged teams and the geriatrics. He stood for a moment and viewed some of the practice matches. An unbiased witness to the testament of lost youth. His neutrality waned, for reasons that defied scrutiny, and he soon found himself rooting for one half of the same team. A flurry of goals from his chosen opposition led Michael to lose interest.

The only thing missing from this walk, thought Michael, was a dog.

Declan Treanor

Dogs and other animals

Michael decided he wanted a dog. Well, he had a dog back on earth-one but he wanted one here. All animals made it over. All animals except the platypus, obviously. Nobody knew why. There were whole populous that dedicated their lives to finding out the answer. Attempting to track otter and duck numbers to see if there was an increase. This was as futile as it was impossible as they did not have the full data set from world-one, and never would. Some believed it was because the platypus should not have existed in the first place.

His earth-one dog was from Bosnia. When Michael and Darren were first looking at getting a dog, they both agreed that it needed to be a rescue dog. Darren had agreed this more than Michael. They had visited a couple of Dogs Homes in the local area and even been introduced to one of the dogs, a lovely little spaniel called 'Buster'. Unfortunately for Michael and Darren during the process of introduction it had snapped at one of the workers. They needed to withdraw their application as at the time Darren's niece was a regular visitor to their home. She was six years old. They thought it prudent to explore other options. Then, just when they were on the cusp of losing momentum, Darren came across an advert for rescue dogs. These were Street dogs. They had been rounded up by the authorities in Bosnia and were due to be culled.

The charity brought them to the UK. Because these dogs had not been mistreated, they were ideal for small children. The dogs had just been knocking around the streets, scavenging food, with not a care in the world. They were in. They travelled over to Worcester that weekend. This was Darren's dog. Darren's dog that Michael walked every evening when Darren was at work.

-

On secondworld humans got 23 years and animals got their own equivalence. For instance, a medium sized dog would get nearly 3 years. If your dog was an adult pedigree and you knew exactly when they had arrived at secondworld, then you would be able to calculate, to the day, when they would pass on again. If they were a mixed breed it took a bit more working out, but it was still fairly accurate. Some sectors had volunteer networks in order to round-up and re-home stray pets, but for a significant part of the population they did not adopt a pet, the pet adopted them. You could be awoken in the middle of the night by a dog standing over you, unable to find its owner, and searching comfort from you instead. Though not uncommon it was better than the shock of waking up with a naked octogenarian in your bed; though admittedly you would be less shocked than the person that had just joined secondworld.

Cats held allegiance to houses; not owners. As far as they were concerned if you were in their house you were obligated to feed them, and woe betide anyone who had a different take on the situation. A budgerigar may appear in your lounge one day but could be easily solved with an open window.

The Kingdomers were traditionally from farming stock. This was why they tended not to eat horses, or cats, or dogs; not for sentimental reasons, the sentiment would come later. No, it was purely because these animals were more useful alive. They worked for the farmer. If you ate your horse, where was your transport, who would pull your plough? Eat the cat and get overrun with rats and mice. The dog was protection and later for herding and fetching. With those that did not have this structure in place they saw the cur as a nuisance, a pest, dangerous and disease carrying.

During the Industrial Revolution traditional farming methods on world-one were replaced with steam-powered mills and threshing machines. Though this was also true of secondworld the motives were worlds apart. Secondworld was trying to give time back to the farmers, trying to improve their standard of living whilst ensuring that there were adequate supplies for the nation and beyond.

There was not the stranglehold led by profits. There were no 'butter mountains', nor any 'milk lakes'. One thing that secondworld struggled to control, however, was the production of beef. A cow killed on world-one appeared in secondworld. This could not change. Due to the amount of beef consumed on world-one, secondworld could not just allow the cattle to roam free as the sheer numbers would overrun the population.

Generally, abattoirs were built on the sites of abattoirs, but this did not solve the excess production of beef. There was more than the Kingdom needed; even with free worldwide distribution the issue was not solved. Most countries were having similar problems with the over farming of animals, the ones that did not were provided for many times over. Added to this was a newfound respect for all life and an increase in vegetarianism and veganism in secondworld.

The thinktanks converged and a solution was tabled. As many animals as possible would be set free; there would be no battery farming and all meat production would be humane; Temple Grandin abattoirs would be sited to match some of their world-one counterparts; after free exports were saturated the remaining meats would be disposed of in the ocean. As a result of the repopulation of prey into the wild, the mountains and forests once again became populous with bears and wolves and lynx and eagles and owls and boars and snakes. But it was the oceans where the real impact was made. The meat was pulped and mixed with grain and the locations of disposal were targeted as best they could. The seas had already benefitted from the world-one trawlers, the catch dying on the boat and replenishing the waters of secondworld, but this was something else. The oceans teemed with life.

Michael's dog was called 'Dario'.

Karl, the rest of his team, and the robots that he likes and who are his pets and that he has named

"Marian!" Karl called.
"What?" replied Marian who was trying to read her book.
"Can I drive one of the times?" Karl asked.
"No." came the curt reply.
"Why not?"
"You do the leaflets… You like doing the leaflets." Marian peeped over the cover.
"Nobody ever reads the leaflets."
Marian used her index finger to mark her page and momentarily closed her book. She wanted to give the illusion that she was giving this matter her full attention. "But you still like doing them, don't you?"
He did like doing them. He held up a bit of sandwich for Sigma to beg for. The robot sat and lifted its front legs off the ground. Karl patted Sigma on the head. "I do like doing them, but we could swap now and again." He dropped a piece of his sandwich into the robot's mouth.
Marian opened up her book again. "Don't do that, it just ends up dropping it all over the floor."
This was true. This Karl knew. But what was also true was that 'Mu' the floor vacuum was doing his rounds and would clean it up as soon as it was dropped.

There were 4 response teams allocated to the South Mid quadrant. The idea was that the operation should run 24hours a day, but the reality was very much dependant on staffing. This was the jurisdiction Karl was assigned to. The teams would work the area, three on response, one on standby. The duties would rotate mid-shift and also on a weekly basis. Karl hated being on standby. This meant it was less likely that you would see anyone but your team members. His team members already knew about secondworld so what on earth was he supposed to talk to them about? Karl would hear his teammates prattling amongst themselves from time to time, but really could not grasp why they opted for such topics of conversation. Football this, boob-tube that. Nonsense.

Declan Treanor

Karl did not really want to drive the truck. In reality he could take one for a spin at any time. There were lots of them in the yard on charge, he could take his pick. He had just mentioned the truck so that he had something to talk about but the conversation had not lasted as long as he had hoped. He was bored.

On the response team they would generally loop the city waiting for a call in, or a register from one of the hospitals or once in a blue moon from the flight nets. Per shift, per team they would average out about four or so cases. With explaining the basics and clerking them in it usually ticked along quite nicely. Some days there was hardly anything, at other times chaos.

But on standby they just sat and waited. No patrols. They were on nights again.

Not many calls registered on the flight nets. Your team may get one during your entire time on the job. They were rare; very rare. Rare but oddly mundane. The nets covered the flight paths of all the commercial aircraft for world-one. On the surface it seemed like a logical step. World-one had planes; people died on planes; if they firstdied on a plane then they would need to catch them to prevent seconddeath. Logical. Firstly, not that many people died on planes. It was, after all, the safest way to travel. But what about a plane crash? If there was a plane crash, at the time of the crash, the plane is generally off course. Okay, let's say you have a heart attack mid-flight. Due to terminal velocity, there was not a vast difference between falling from 500 feet or from 20,000 feet but the nets still needed to be under the person. You would need the pilot to be flying on the exact proposed trajectory, with an altitude that was conducive to being caught mid-air in a net. If the stars align, and luck and fortune hold hands for a while, you catch someone in the flight net. Whoop-de-do! You get them down and take them to get processed; same as everyone else.

Karl's attention went back to his robots.

Karl loved the little robots. His favourite was 'Sigma'. Karl had named all 27 of the robots at the Processing Hub. They had initially gone by product code, and then by assignment number but Karl thought this was disrespectful to the robots. On one level Karl understood that these robots had no AI functionality, had no feelings about their names, and had no feelings whatsoever; and he was also conscious of the fact that these 'tricks' he had taught the robots were just programmes that he himself had laboriously imputed. He knew all this, but he liked to pretend.

None of the robots in Kingdom had AI functionality. This had been agreed in principle when the mere concept of Artificial Intelligence was first introduced. It was deemed unethical to create something of intelligence for a role of bondage. The Foundation for the Protection of Artificial Intelligence was created. Karl had once watched the current head of the organisation, Arthur C Clarke, give a talk on the subject. "Here we are trying to create a life, something that is intellectually superior in many ways, and we want it to be subservient, obligated to perform menial tasks on our say-so. Our whims catered for by cerebral giants. Do we really want to chain this creation before its realisation? Born into servitude."

Even if you struggled with the ethics of the issue, common sense prevailed. Why would you need the mundane to be performed by an Einstein? Robots had their place. Robots could do the things humans did not want to do, monotonous tasks, dangerous tasks. AI's would have their evolution separate to the duties of man. Both flourished. Now that the distinction was made, and the line drawn, it gave protection to any AI. They could not be exploited. This did not, however, mean that the AI was limited to the ethereal; the ghost in the machine. They were, now the distinction was made, open to exploit the use of robotics to their own end. They were able to create and utilise robots in order to serve their own needs, be this to further some aspect of a research project, to complete a task that they required to be completed, or merely to give themselves a form in order to better understand the world and their place in it. Compassion as a concept, in its purest form.

They were calling for people to be compassionate about an idea, something that wasn't by definition a life; compassionate about potential. It was absolutely the right thing to do, but probably the main reason that the protections continued to be observed was the sneaking suspicion of what may happen if you mistreated AI, fuelled by countless sci-fi books and films. Some cautious people said thank you to their 'Alexa' for that very reason. These concerns were a long way from being manifest, currently AI amounted to a very large and very quick search engine.

Karl stopped dropping bits of sandwich into the metal pincers at the front end of the robotic unit and patted it on its payload port.

While Karl fussed Sigma, and Marian read her book, Paul and Paul played chess. Paul was medium height, medium build and bald. He had begun to bald in world-one and had thought to himself 'two can play at that game'. He shaved his head and continued to do so when he came to secondworld, though if truth be known he would now have a full head of hair if left to its own devices. His white shirt contrasted starkly with his ebony skin. Paul was stocky and was slightly taller than Paul. He secretly missed having a missing finger and the scar that once adorned his face. They had offered to teach the others how to play chess, but Marian had politely declined, and Karl had declined.

Prior to their chess game the Paul's had already completed the shift checklists. The mobile units had sufficient resources and were responding to walkie-talkie checks; there were no alerts from the hospitals or care homes. The hospitals had their own skeleton staff, mainly admin and first responders. The older adult placements usually had good staffing levels as they were obliged to offer continued accommodation. The vast majority of former residents, however, did not take them up on the offer as their rejuvenated bodies gave them a new lease of life.
The motorised life jackets were charged, and lakes were clear; they had put all the trucks that were not in use on charge and the flight nets were tracking and responding. The flight nets in some regions fell into disrepair and due to the rarity of their successful use there were not many that noticed. The thought of getting rid of them altogether was unpalatable but a working solution to fix the air travel issue had yet to be addressed. That said, the Paul's made sure their nets did not fall into disrepair. The job was a commitment, and the Paul's took that commitment seriously. They all did. They all had their reasons for taking on the role and all had their plans to get out. They were not financially bound to the job, no one was. But unlike world-one, the realisation that life was short and that there was more to life than this job would not come too late as they all had the reminder stamped on their arm.

It was generally agreed that if you died as a singular, you moved on, spouse-wise that is. If you died it was considered bad-form to wish your spouse dead, though this might be from a place of good intent. Whilst you may want to see them again, wishing them to take an early bath was frowned upon in polite society. This was somewhat dictated by your age of course. If you were 98 and your partner a similar age, you might want to hold on for a bit before you started to build a whole new life.

Paul had arrived after his wife died; she had already moved on, but they remained close. He would go to theirs for dinner every third Sunday. Whereas Paul's wife was still on world-one. Paul had smoked himself to death. He had always said 'you've got to die of something' with the follow-up 'it might as well be slow and painful'.

Paul had 'seen it all' during his time as a Midwife. People terrified; people elated. People who were already resident to secondworld lying on the floor naked, as a prank.

Gallows humour, normally a prerequisite for this type of role, was not required on secondworld. The death was a rebirth and so could be celebrated as such.

But that did not mean he had not also witnessed tragedy.

One incident that remained with him was a building fire on world-one causing three deaths. This was fairly standard procedure for the Midwives. Paul attended with his team at the time. Go in, get the three new arrivals and get them in the van. The thing was that during the fire, the building on world-one suffered a partial collapse. This caused the building on world-one to fall out of sync with the secondworld building. One of the people was transported right into the structure of the building. Paul never talked about it, and tried not to think about it, but often failed. The chess helped.

The replication of world-one was habit born of necessity. People learned the hard way to avoid creating secondworld structures that did not exist on world-one. Once witnessed, you would not want to see again the results of someone materialising into a wall.

Declan Treanor

Mirror man

He sat. The room dimly lit. In front of him, a mirror.

He knew well the reflection that looked back at him. His breathing steady.

He wished for no distractions.

He focussed on the pupil of the right eye, the eye that stared back at him.

He held his own gaze. He waited.

The iris blackened. He blinked and the image reset.

He focused again on the pupil of the right eye.

He waited.

The left side of his face began to melt. The flesh sagging and his eyelid drooping to expose the occupied socket.

He fought the desire to refocus but could not prevent it. His face snapped back to normality.

He went again. This time the effects began sooner.

His head began to swell, from the right side initially, then the left. His jaw elongated.

Something slithered behind him on the wall.

The reflections eyes looked away from him momentarily, then back.

The image then smiled, showing its teeth. It held a rictus grin.

Then, in a moment, it was gone. There was no reflection at all.

He scrambled away from the mirror in a blind panic.

The contorted images of his own face could not hold the same fear. The fear of there being nothing.

Declan Treanor

Welcome to Secondworld Carol

Carol died in hospital. Prior to her death she had fallen in and out of consciousness, so to come to in a hospital bed was not too disconcerting. The room on secondworld was very similar albeit a starker version. None of her cards, or personal items were there, none of her family were there, and she was naked underneath the bedsheets. It was also odd that the bedsheets appeared to be on some sort of raised frame. She guessed it was the night due to limited lighting and the quietness of the ward.

Physically, Carol was feeling a lot better. She looked around for some clothing and spotted a hospital gown folded on the chair next to her bed. Pushing back the bedsheet frame Carol dressed herself and went out into the corridor. "Hullooo" she uttered softly but musically. She startled the nurse who was positioned at the nursing station and apologised for doing so. The nurse exchanged light-hearted pleasantries with Carol before suggesting that Carol return to bed and she would bring her a cup of tea. The nurse also said something about alerting the team to her presence, but Carol wasn't quite sure what that meant.

Carol was met by the Midwives and duly processed. She was informed that her husband had preceded her by 12 days and that she would be accommodated with him unless she had any objections. She did not.

As the reality of her situation took hold Carol began to weep. She wept for the child she left behind. The bereavement was hers not his. She would likely not see him again. She desperately wanted him here with her but wanted more that he lived a long and full life. To have lived two full lives. She wanted everything for him but mostly wanted to console him. She wanted to tell him that mommy and daddy were fine, that he would be fine. She wanted to hold him one last time, to let him know that he was loved and would be loved from afar. She mourned her loss and wept for his pain.

The PO did her best to console Carol but knew from experience that it would take time. When the processing was completed the transport team was summoned.

Carol had managed to compose herself somewhat before the transport team arrived. Her mind was racing as they left the depot, or it was attempting to race but was being tripped up by the most talkative man she had ever met. "…which leaves gaps, cos with the trauma gone you …" She attempted to zone out. "…except for platypuses, which may seem weird but …" Carol continued to ignore the fellow and looked out of the window in another vain attempt to gather her thoughts. "Nice bloke, not very chatty, but nice. Not sure how you feel about him, him causing the accident an all."

"Sorry?" Carol responded, suddenly becoming aware of the content of this man's ramblings.

"I was the one who greeted him; the fella that caused your crash. The one that killed you and your husband. Lovely bloke. Bit quiet." The man met Carol's eyes. "I can give you his address if you want."

-

Carol approached the front door and knocked gingerly. Unbeknownst to her, her husband Brian had been notified of her death while she was being processed; shortly after she had confirmed that she wanted to renew contact with her partner. Brian threw open the door and embraced Carol. They held each other for some moments before the Midwife excused himself and returned to his vehicle. They held each other still. Brian only loosened the embrace to shower Carol with kisses. Nothing was said. Brian held up Carol's face to meet his, so that he could look into her eyes. They held each other's stare until new tears formed. Carol buried her head into his shoulder. Nothing needed to be said. Eventually Brian took Carol by the hand and led her into the apartment. He closed the door behind them.

Transcendence

"I can't help the way I feel." Brian chanced.
"Can't help the way you feel!? You can't help the way you feel? But you can help the way you act! 'Can't help the way you feel?', as if it has nothing to do with you. You have no control over your own mind, no control over the way you behave. It's just an excuse, and a bad one at that."
She paused for breath.
"You can't!" Carol was enraged. "I've never heard anything so stupid in all my life!"
Brian looked at her dolefully. Silent.
"You just can't!" Carol was standing over a seated Brian. "And what am I supposed to do?"

Brian knew better than to answer. Carol collapsed into the armchair opposite. She craned her face heavenward; eyes darting across the ceiling.
"Tell them you've changed your mind." She looked at Brian, he was looking down. "Don't do this, don't leave me." Her voice was softer now but still pained.
"Then come with me." Brian's voice was barely a whisper. "We can wait in the Fifth Realm together. We can wait for our boy."
Carol looked at her hands and attempted to keep her tone measured. "How can you believe this nonsense? You're talking about killing yourself. Killing yourself for some cult. How are you buying into this shit?" Her gaze looked up to meet his. His wet eyes betrayed him. She doubted that he believed what he was saying, he just didn't have the strength to go on.

-

Carol was a bright, fun person. She was annoying to all, but the playful kind of annoying. People adored being annoyed by her and she was more than happy to oblige. She was joy personified.

Brian loved her deeply. He was more seriously minded than Carol, but you would be hard pushed to find anyone less serious. Their joy only magnified when they were blessed with their son. They shared the load and basked in the glow of sleep deprivation. They were each other's worlds. Work and bills and chores and taxes meant nothing. The love that they had for each other, and the hope they had for the future made them impervious to the drudgery of day-to-day life.

To have that ripped away. She felt it in the core of her. They had lost their boy, and she would never see him again. She prayed with all her might and to whoever was listening that she would never see him again. This was perhaps even more cruel a fate. She could feel the longing of wanted to hold him once more but needed to stamp on the feeling. She needed to crush any yearning or hint of a wish. If any part of an unknown deity was eavesdropping, she could never forgive her wish being granted. Now he was leaving her too, but she understood. She could not forgive him. She could not blame him. She understood but had no intention of following suit. She would navigate her suffering. She would think about her boy every day. She would think about them both. She would write to her boy and tell him of all the great adventures she had, and the people she had met, and that she lived a life worth living, and she would let him know that he was loved. Her life would be lived in honour of his.

-

Brian completed his Transcendence Ritual the following day. Carol went with him, resigned to his decision. Brian chose a dignified end. Simple yet dignified. Carol did not watch him die, she could not. But she stayed until he closed his eyes. She kissed him gently and left the room in tears.

She had lost so much in such a short period of time. Her heart had been wrenched and torn at. The tattered remains were just enough to remind her of her pain. Her throat contained a constant knot.

The room she had only just begun to know seemed so very empty on her return that day.

-

It was some days later that Carol came across the paper with Michael's address on it. It was folded inside the leaflet she had been given. She had almost forgotten about it. Would she try and find Michael? After all, she did have a message for him.

Declan Treanor

Dark Clouds

Michael was getting the hang of secondworld. He enjoyed the pace of life that Nesfield-upon-Hean afforded him. He would go for walks, prepare food, read. He would take a stroll through the village, do odd jobs for those that needed them done, and would meet up with Victor often. He had developed a taste for brandy and thought that this would keep him warm in the winter. What would he do without Victor? The time was fast approaching. What time did Victor have left? It would not be long now. Today Michael was going on a hike.

As he walked through the vast fields, the tall grass swayed gently in the breeze, and the sun hung high in the clear, blue sky. Michael felt the warmth of the sunlight on his face, and a sense of tranquillity washed over him. The countryside stretched out before him, with rolling hills and distant trees dotting the landscape.

Michael marvelled at the peacefulness that enveloped him. Birds chirped and screeched overhead, and the distant hum of insects provided a soothing soundtrack to his journey. He found himself immersed in the natural rhythms of the countryside, where the passing of time was marked by the sun's journey across the sky.

Michael wondered what time it was so held up his hand to the sky. This was something that was second nature to him now. There were signposts when leaving the village illustrating how to do this so that people going on hikes were able to work out, and action, their return journey before nightfall. You could get a watch if you wanted but Michael did not feel the need. There was a clock in his apartment and if he was in the village the church would give you the time both with display and chimes. Michael counted the number of fingers from the horizon to the sun. He reckoned he had about an hour and forty-five left. Satisfied with his rough estimate, he continued his leisurely stroll, taking in the beauty of the countryside.

As he meandered through the fields, the landscape transformed with the shifting angles of sunlight. Shadows lengthened, and the colours of the flora intensified. Michael felt a deep connection to the earth beneath his feet and the vast expanse stretching out before him.

Eventually, as the sun began its descent, casting a warm and golden hue over the fields, he reached a peaceful spot. He decided to sit and enjoy the spectacle of the sunset. The sky transformed into a canvas of oranges, pinks, and purples, and the man couldn't help but feel grateful for the simplicity of this moment— the beauty of nature unfolding in its own timeless rhythm.

Behind him, to the east, dark clouds were forming.

-

Michael quickened his pace as the rain began to fall. As he advanced on his apartment he saw a figure sitting down in the doorway. They were sat with their knees to their chest and their arms wrapped around their shins. At first he thought they were just using the porch canopy for shelter but as he approached the person called out their name. "Michael? Michael Slater?" Michael slowed his pace but continued to move steadily forward. The lady brought herself to her feet. "Hi. Are you Michael Slater?"

"Yes." Replied Michael. Some of his residual world-one scepticism remained, but he saw no reason to deny such a fact.

"Ah, good. Can we talk?" The lady stepped aside to allow Michael to unlock the door and stepped inside when directed to do so.

-

"Should he be giving out peoples addresses?" Michael was a little perturbed, not at the appearance of Carol, but at the complete lack of regard Karl had for GDPR.

"It's fine apparently. Or at least that's what the man told me." Carol assured Michael as she attempted to dry her hair with the towel he had provided "He said if I wasn't allowed contact with you, that they would have been informed, and they hadn't been informed, so it was probably alright."

"Mmmm." Michael wasn't convinced but decided to let it go for the time being as he was still none the wiser about the reason for Carols visit. He had first been distracted by trying to accommodate Carol in an attempt to dry herself and then sidetracked by the news that Karl was indeed a blabbermouth.

"Sorry Carol, do we know each other? From before? My memory hasn't been great since I got here." Michael placed a cup of tea next to Carol and returned to the kitchen area to retrieve his own.

"No, we don't really know each other as such. But we have ran into each other before." Carol did not want to admit to herself that she had prepared that response. "We were in the same car crash."

"Oh!" replied Michael. It hadn't occurred to him before that others may have died in the same crash. He pondered this new information. "I didn't see you on the road. The day I got here I mean, when I turned up on secondworld."

"No. You wouldn't have; I only got here last week. Surprised you didn't see my husband though. Saying that, I'm not sure if he died on the scene or not." Carol's overall tone was nonchalant, but a slight timbre was present in her voice when she spoke of her husband.

"Christ! Look Carol, I really am sorry. I don't know what to say. I don't know what happened that morning. Is your husband okay?"

Carol ignored Michael's question. That was not why she was here. She did not want to inflict further supplementary distressing revelations on this man as she had not unburdened herself of the primary one yet. She also doubted if she had the strength to vocalise that still raw event. "I have something to tell you about that day. You might want to sit down."

Hush

Carol had been admitted to hospital following the crash, this she knew. She could recall beeping monitors and the rhythmic whoosh of a ventilator. The faint scent of antiseptic. She felt her mouth and throat full. At times Carol was lucid enough to be aware of people around her. People sat by her bedside, her parents. Her father, his voice etched with worry and grief. He held her hand as if it were a lifeline. The medical team, spoke in hushed tones, their discussions veiled in the language of charts and medical jargon. Nurses paced the room, doctors lingered near the doorway. Her mother, a gentle woman, silent and unconsolable.

Meanwhile, Carol lay still, her mind alert within the confines of her motionless body. She could hear the doctors' conversations, the measured tones that hinted at difficult decisions. A strange feeling of detachment took over Carol. She understood that she would likely die in that room and though her heart yearned for her son she had accepted her fate. On reflection this may have been down to the copious amount of drugs being pumped into her.

In this state of limbo, without the ability to communicate, Carol became bored with the tragedy of her own story. She took to listening to the TV. There were gameshows and soap operas but the fact that her crash was on the news was of obvious interest.

First came the reports of a pileup on the motorway where two people were killed. Carol recognised that this was the crash that she had been in. Two dead, that was horrendous. She supposed she was the one they referred to when they said one in critical condition. She felt quite lucid at these times but also recognised that she was fading in and out of consciousness. As the story progressed it moved from the local news to the national news and soon began to dominate all the news coverage. She learned that she was indeed the one in critical condition but also that her husband had died. It only occurred to her after the news of his death that he had not visited her in hospital. She was sorry that her husband had died but was more concerned about her son. He would have no one now, as she had already accepted her fate. She would have cried if she could have.

The crash and the deaths were newsworthy enough but now a man had been helping police with their enquiries. There was speculation about what this could possibly mean, given the circumstances, with reporters and experts walking the tightrope of libelous comments and public interest. The man was subsequently arrested, and his identity revealed.

"It was your husband Michael, they arrested your husband." Carol left time for the information to be processed.
"Are you sure?" Michael's mind was a fog. He was glad that he had taken the advice from Carol to sit down.
"Yes. Very sure." Carol replied and took a deep breath. "The next part I am not so sure about because some of the reports were conflicting... and, ya know, the drugs and the brain damage and stuff." She steadied herself but looked at the floor when she spoke again. "They think he might have killed you, poisoned you or something, which caused the crash." Carol looked up and met Michaels eyes. "I know you don't know me from Adam and I know this is a lot. I mean, a lot! But I thought it best come from me. I haven't told anyone else, not even the people at the start, the ones who ask all the questions. I thought it better if you heard it from me." She smiled an awkward smile. "Though I'm beginning to doubt that now."

Michael collected himself enough to remember his manners. "No, not at all. Thank you for letting me know." He attempted to gather his thoughts that were jumping and spilling out all over the place.

Carol stood up, her chair squealing as it was forced backwards. "Right. I'd better head off."

"Please stay." Michael was shocked by his own response, but when he poked at it, it held up. He did want her to stay. He was unsure why. Maybe a million reasons. But one of them was that he did not want to be alone with this news. Even if they did not mention it again, Michael wanted to be around someone who shared this knowledge. "I can put the kettle on, and we can just chat...., chat about anything. Anything you like."

Carol sat back down. "Okay. That would be nice." In reality Carol thought that neither of them had much small talk in them, but it may be nice to concentrate on someone else's big stuff, even just for a little while. As the kettle boiled Carol thought about her final moments in that hospital.

Carol, in the stillness of her silent existence, yearned to comfort her loved ones and yearned to see her boy once more. She longed to tell them that she understood, that they could release her from the tethers of the machines that sustained her fragile existence. Yet, she remained a prisoner within her own body, a silent observer to the unfolding drama of life and death.

In the stillness that followed, Carol felt a strange sense of liberation. The weight that bound her dissipated, and as the last echoes of the machines faded away, she embraced the quiet peace that enveloped her. And in the corners of the room, her loved ones grappled with the bittersweet truth that love, even in its most painful form, demanded the courage to let go.

When she thought of her son she only thought of joy. It was a sad and painful joy. A joy that could tear you apart.

Michael thought too.

He needed meat on the bones of this. Why would he be targeted, and who by? If Carol was to be believed it seemed he had been drugged or poisoned. Not that Carol had any reason to lie, he thought, but she could well have been mistaken.

Any drugs surely would have been detected when he died, regardless of the circumstances. They would have tested him to rule out whether he had been drinking or using illicit substances, wouldn't they? That was normal practice he was sure, if the police dramas that Darren forced Michael to watch were anything to go by.

Was the car crash a gruesome side effect of his murder, or the mode of execution. His husband had been arrested; had he been charged? Darren was not stupid. If it was him, he must have known he would be found out, but who else would have a motive? 'Who else?' What was he saying? Darren didn't even have a motive. The questions intrigued Michael, but he was not outraged. No sense of injustice captured him. It was somehow less important now that he knew what death entailed. Maybe Darren did

Declan Treanor

kill him, it's usually the spouse. He couldn't think of a valid reason though. He thought they were happy.

Murder a crow

It was perhaps inevitable that death occupied his thoughts. He had, after all, recently died himself.

After Carol left a sunken memory popped up from the depths. He hadn't thought about this in years and wasn't sure why this had presented itself now.

Michael was never quite sure about the 'putting it out of its misery' thing. Yes, an animal may be in pain but would pain not be more acceptable than non-existence. If the being was able to communicate its preference, that would be preferable. But to make the decision for them. Especially physical pain. Physical pain was always better than psychological pain, he thought. So, you come across an animal in physical pain, or are called to an animal in distress. More often than not the person doing the summoning had something to do with the reason the animal is in pain in the first place. I've hit an animal with my car, I feel bad about it, I now want you to kill it. Is that how it goes?

Michael could remember such a situation on world-one. He had received a frantic call from one of his neighbours. They had exchanged numbers 'in case of an emergency' but the calls were always in one direction. On this particular occasion there was a crow in her front garden. It had been mauled by something or other, most probably her cat. It was in a dreadful state. She wanted him to put it out of its misery. Was it cruel to leave the animal in distress? He assessed the being. Its neck was torn open. Strands of itself intertwined with the lawn that was due a cut. The claret strands mixed with the green blades. Unidentifiable blobs of purple. If he could perhaps mend it, nurse it to health he may have tried but that was not an option. The mass of feathers throbbed. Pulsated.

He complied with his neighbours wishes without vocalising or intimating any internal ethical wrangling. He requested a shovel which was fetched and brought to him. He placed the cutting edge of the shovel's blade across the remainder of the neck and positioned his foot upon the step. For a moment he stood, one legged, hovering over the crow, ready to dispatch. Measuring himself so that he would be able to unleash enough pressure to do this cleanly. To ensure that his proposition was such that the animal did not suffer.

Again, a pang of guilt. Was the bird capable of reflection? He thought not. He doubted the bird was looking back on its fledgling days, but did this allow him to decide that this current life was one that needed to be extinguished? He did not know. But he did know that his neighbour was upset by this dying animal, and that inaction may have been misconstrued as queasiness, or worse, cowardice; and he knew also the saying 'to put it out of its misery'. So that is what he did. He leaned his full weight onto the shovel and through the blade. The shovel cut through the crow and into the lawn. There was a crunch. The deed was done. Maybe it was the right thing to do.

Now that he had died himself, the moment sat better with him.

Innocent

Michael donned boots and light raincoat. He was going to see the Bureau today. He was unsure how you went about investigating a murder across time but maybe they would know, or at least point him in the right direction. Was it 'across time' he thought idly to himself. World-one was keeping the same time as them, or at least he assumed that to be the case. They say world-one and secondworld but it's the same place really, just another dimension maybe!? Again, another assumption but it seemed to fit. A cross-dimensional investigation was what was needed.

Carol said she would go with him, and he felt that it was proper. She was alone now, and this may give her some sense of purpose or at the very least a distraction.

The Government in the Kingdom still had the head of state, but this was more of an administrative role. They were there to collate the findings of the various Thinktanks and rule on any matters that were in dispute. The Thinktanks were tasked with different projects including transport, education, midwifery, robotics, world-one contact, environment, the meaning of life, or any number of new task-and-finish groups. In 1853 party politics had been abolished and since then the country had never run so efficiently.

If you so wished, you could be part of the Government. An application was made, and you were either elected or rejected by the Bureau. Most were accepted. Previous experience was undesirable but did not exclude you from the process.

Pen pushers were pushed out. The bureaucracy lovers were allowed to form committees without teeth. The system could not be influenced, and nobody was really that keen to do so. The social standing and social drivers were no longer there. There was no grease for the palms.

The public were canvassed, but this was no way meant as a referendum. It was the think-tanks job to look into the detail and make the call. Why would you expect those not in government to do their job for them. Ridiculous.

A lot of the pressure points that were experienced in world-one were just not present in secondworld, this negated the need for the political animal and lost was the platform to foster discontent and disillusionment. Healthcare; barring accidents everyone was fit and well. Immigration; there was lots of room for all, now that everyone had a modest living space. Cost of living crisis? What cost of living crisis?

If you had a problem, you went to the Bureau and if they couldn't solve it, they took it to the Think-tanks.

There was a shadow government still, but their role was purely to rudder. To police the government, ensure corruption was not sneaking back in, to steady the course.

As there was little chance for corruption the roles were often less desirable to those who had trod this path before. Whatever sense of entitlement that was felt was quickly washed away when the subject learned of how the Government was governed. Quicker than the tide at Morecambe Bay, a statement was released to say that they wished to pursue other things. Nobody had asked them to make a statement, nobody expected a statement, and nobody read the statement once it was issued. This was purely a hangover from the days when they believed themselves to be more important than everyone else. Once the reality of the way this new world worked took hold, introspection followed. A re-evaluation of their moral compass took place. Either that or they moved to the Southern Union States.

Michael found the department and who he needed to contact. Innocent Baba was the regional official that headed, amongst other things, crime.

-

Innocent was not a short figure, but the shape of his hair made him seem much taller than he was. The consistency of his afro-textured hair enabled it to be sculptured into a tricorn design. There were three fins, one in the centre, the other two flanking the sides, making his head look like a rocket-ship mid-flight. The rest of the scalp was shaved bald. It would have been considered to have been quite contemporary had this not been a traditional Rwandan hairstyle. He wore a crisp white shirt, and off-white sarong. A pencil thin moustache teetered on his top lip.

Carol made note of the sarong. 'I bet he's all mouth and no trousers.' she mused and smiled to herself. She logged the joke with the hope to crowbar it into a future conversation. She very much hoped that there would be little substance to what the man said but felt a twinge of guilt at choosing the mechanics of a joke over support for her newfound friend. Guilt aside, she stuck by her decision.

She watched him peel the orange. He was doing it weird. She couldn't quite figure out what was strange about it at first. Was it just that she had not seen anyone peel an orange in a while? No, there was something else. He was peeling it north to south! As far as she could recall, she could remember people doing the long strands whilst rotating the orange, or when the orange was bloated the technique of nipping little discs of skin from the body. Not only was he peeling it in the wrong direction he was now stopping intermittently to remove a segment. He was obviously doing this for effect. She now saw that he saw that she was watching him peel the orange.

"So how can I help?" Innocent opened.

"I'm not sure you can." Admitted Michael honestly. "But it looks like I might have been killed."

Michael and Carol took it in turns to explain their current understanding of the situation whilst Innocent demonstrated his 'active listening' skills by interjecting at appropriate times. "I see." He would say. "Naturally." Or "Quite, quite." Innocent had been on a course and understood the importance of pretending to listen.

When the couple had completed their story Innocent sat back in his chair. "This is indeed quite the remarkable story. Yes, quite remarkable, but I am not sure that there is anything that can be done." Both Michael and Carol had guessed this may have been the case, but they were still crestfallen when their suspicions were confirmed. Innocent continued. "Look. I will relay this tale to my police officer in the hope that she can offer a solution."

'Police Officer!?' Michael thought to himself 'singular?'. Michael and Carol thanked Innocent for his time and stood up to leave.

"Is there any way we can be told if more information comes to light?" Carol chanced.

"You could go to the Processing Hub I suppose. I doubt there would be any other crash victims but there might be people that followed the news story. Best I can do I'm afraid." They had caught Innocent off guard, and he had been unintentionally helpful.

That was not a bad idea, Michael thought, and they were all out of ideas. "I'm going to go over to the Processing Hub." Michael told Carol.

"I'll go with you. I tell the story better." Carol replied. She left a pause. "That Innocent bloke. All mouth and no trousers!"

"Absolutely." Responded Michael a beat too soon.

'Damn' thought Carol, he didn't get it. Given the gravitas of the situation she prevented herself from forcing Michael to recognise the pun. She hoped that the man wore sarongs often and the chance to recycle this joke would present itself in the not-too-distant future. She may add 'literally' to the end of it the next time.

The Welcome Book

Before he retired to bed Michael got out the Welcome Book again. He had made good progress with this, though had still not managed to read the leaflet he had been given on his first day. It was around here somewhere, but he could not think for the life of him where.

Michael had already read about 'The Great Indian Famine'; C. S. Lewis; and the intriguing case of 'the Death of Hopscotch.'

He scanned the contents and dipped in and out of the different topics. Some passages were very short, just giving a few lines, some were more in-depth.

Michael dipped his toe into the French Revolution and found it was one of the few cases where the newly dead lost out. The Monarchy that passed over, it seemed, were unrepentant and cared not for a redressing of past sins. Those that faced the guillotine faced it twice that day. Once clothed, once naked.

'Figures of Note' was an interesting section. He supposed that he could look up a specific person if he attacked the index, but on a quick flick through made him wonder who was selecting which people and why.

Barbara Cartland jumped off the page. Apparently, she just kept writing. On her arrival to secondworld Dame Cartland accepted her modest surroundings but did insist on the décor being addressed. Once established she produced her first secondworld based bodice-ripper within a month. Proof indeed that this was what she was put on the earths to do. It was more than enjoyment, though she did enjoy her work, it was her reason for being. Her ikigai. She could not imagine doing anything else and she was eternally grateful to have been given the opportunity to continue. With her extended years she produced a further 328 books. It would have been more but with her health restored she also began gliding as a hobby.

Bela Lugosi spent a year contemplating whether, essentially, running about in a cape and false teeth was a worthwhile and fitting use of a life. After some deep contemplation on the matter, he decided that it was indeed, and that he would spend his remaining 22 years doing the same. It was universally agreed, give or take one or two people, that he had made the correct evaluation, and that Bela not only lived a life worth living he provided a blueprint for how to live a life worth living. 'He enriched the lives of others to the extent that they felt the warmth and value of existence.'

There seemed to be some bias in the book, and some of the articles were peculiarly worded, but he trusted the book more than he did Victor. Whilst he was very fond of Victor's stories, he worried that some of them may have been exactly that. Stories.

Michael flicked through some more of the chapters. Skim reading and stopping on parts that piqued his interest.

Genghis Khan was apparently worshiped as a God by his enemies. This was prior to him presenting at secondworld and was due to the millions of deaths made under his name. The general consensus was that Chinggis Khan had created their civilisation, had allowed them to be reborn. He was lorded as the God of Life.

When Genghis eventually died, his followers did him the service of helping him to his next encounter. Despite his protestations they insisted that in order to fulfil the prophecy he would be sacrificed. Most stated that they believed the prophecy to be true. Some just wished the man dead but were happy to go along with this.

Pompeii was a double tragedy. The people of Pompeii on earth-one died but the same eruption that killed them was happening on secondworld.

A cruel twist of fate, or a cruel twist of God's design, depending on your outlook.

China had the great flood of Yangtze River which was estimated to have killed 3.7 million people, once in world-one and again in secondworld.

Natural disasters were often, but not always replicated across the worlds. Tectonic plates were rarely influenced by the butterfly effect.

-

The secondworld ancestors, on the whole, set to recreate what once was. Rather, to recreate what still was, but was someplace else. Like homesick travellers they sought to replicate the known.

This was also necessary to protect those being born to secondworld. To have a heart attack in world-one on the 17th floor would be doubly fatal if there was no 17th floor replicated in secondworld.

Though the nuclear shadows of Hiroshima and Nagasaki were not cast on this land. In a flash a population found itself transported to secondworld. Entire families, confused, but together.

This, however, posed quite a unique difficulty. How to replicate the intensive rebuild of Japan without the preceding annihilation? This led to some of the most creative architectural. Michael looked in wonder at some of the pictures displayed in the book.

Skyscrapers towering above the earth, each one holding a part of the traditional Japan underneath- like a forest canopy. The Nagarekawa Methodist Church was cradled by a building that stretched above it. Pagodas and marketplaces enveloped by mighty structures that snaked the Motoyasugawa river. Once the technique of building above buildings was established there was nothing to prevent them from exploiting this empty airspace. A transport infrastructure linking these towers was also built. Electric trains raced above their heads.

Michael closed the book and went to bed, with thoughts of faith, thoughts of hope.

Rain

The morning brought with it the rain. It had started in the early hours and persisted through to midday. As the rain continued its descent, a sense of calm enveloped the village. It was as if time itself slowed down, allowing each raindrop to tell a story of its journey from the clouds to the ground. The patter of rain became a lullaby, cradling Michael in a moment of serenity.

Nature revelled in the downpour, as rivers swelled with newfound energy, and birds took refuge in the sheltering embrace of branches. The rain breathed vitality into the flora and fauna outside and Michael watched through the window. He would brave the rain soon, but for the meantime was content just to view.

He sipped his tea.

The rain patterns competed for his attention. Watching the race of droplets, or the explosive splashes. The ricochet.

'O Superman' by Laurie Anderson came on the radio, or at least a replica of the song. A facsimile. He was suddenly tearful. This took him by surprise. The sadness alarmed him, caught him off guard. Wasn't this supposed to have gone? Surely this was some held trauma!? What was worse was that he had no idea why. The tears were streaming now, pushed up through his chest. He let the tears flow as he stood stock-still in the kitchen looking out at the alley below.

Victor was in the woodland dressed in his Sou'wester hat and oilskin duster, his bow in hand. The scent of rain, both earthy and fresh, permeated the air, releasing the pent-up fragrance of soil and vegetation. It was a perfume that signalled the cleansing of the world, a rejuvenating elixir that promised life to dormant seeds and quenched the thirst of the land.

Rain, a symphony of nature's tears, descended from the heavens, transforming the world below into a glistening tapestry of life, renewal and wet tarmac. The rhythmic percussion of raindrops against the roof of the van created a soothing melody like a jazz fusion steel drum section.

Karl sat looking out through the trucks window, content in his thoughtlessness.

The landscape underwent a transformation. Leaves glistened with droplets, flowers bowed gracefully under the weight of water, and streets gleamed with a reflective sheen. Puddles formed, creating miniature mirrors that mirrored the world above. All of which was ignored by Jackie who was experiencing experiences that were stimulated by stimulants.

In the village, umbrellas bloomed like vibrant flowers, a sea of colourful canopies weaving through the grey landscape. The sound of footsteps against wet pavement added a percussive element to the symphony, as people hurried to find shelter. The feeling of foreboding had taken hold of Florence and its grip tightened on her as she sat attempting to puzzle her way out of this feeling of doom.

Carol looked out and saw it was raining. 'Nuts!' she thought and switched on the boob-tube.

Drink again

Cheap booze was always available. Beer was brewed in cellars, cider was pressed, whiskey stills in potting sheds, bathtub gin, potatoes grown and poteen produced, orange wine in every household. These could be procured for a favour or a song. If you were good company people invited you to soiree's. There would be candlelight and music; food and drink. Bring something if you have something, if you have nothing, bring yourself. Communities getting together. If you wanted your roof fixed, throw a party. First work and then play. If you were not fixing the roof you were helping with the party preparation, if you were not helping with the preparation you brought supplies, if you did not bring supplies you provided entertainment. If you did nothing it was remembered.

Michael didn't really drink in world-one, but he was happy to be in the company of Victor and found himself drinking more often than not now. He also found Victor's arguments for drinking compelling. Victor was currently mid-flow with such an argument.

"Have you seen toddlers; how happy they are? This is the state of oblivion we are seeking. Inter-peace can only bring you so far. Oblivion is the goal." Victor was looking for recruits and excuses for his drinking spree "You can travel the world, seek adrenaline fixes with extreme sports, mix with the great and the good, become appallingly wealthy, have thrilling romances, win awards for excellence in your chosen profession, you will never be as happy as a 2-year-old who has had their nose returned to them after it's theft."

He had not been with Carol to the Bureau today, though this was getting to be somewhat of a routine. They would go and be told there was no news and that there was no point in visiting the Bureau, and that if any news came through, they would contact them. On one occasion they were told that someone came through who had heard about the case but could not expand on what was already known.

Carol would be joining them tonight. She had met Victor once before and while Michael was happy to listen to Victor's monologues without interjection, Carol was not. In their first meeting she had moved from being politely combative, to being openly oppositional for the sake of her own amusement and sanity.

Victor had finished lording the benefits of drink and was now in the throes of explaining why corporal punishment wasn't great to a passive Michael.

"'They made me do it'. Don't they see that that's worse? If you are doing something evil because you don't know any better, or you think you're doing the right thing; or hell, even if you are doing it because you want to do something evil. These are all better reasons. All of them. Because when you say you were made to do it, that means you knew it was wrong, you didn't want to do it, but you did it anyway."

"...and what about salvation? What about forgiveness?" Michael had momentarily zoned out, lost in his own thoughts, thinking about his morning and Victor was now mid-rant about corporal punishment, and the continuation of this practice in what was formally known as America. More accurately, this was America made up of five and a quarter states from their original haul.

Even more accurately Victor was referring to the Southern Union States or SUS. These were some lands that had been generously donated by the indigenous people of Novus Mundus so that western immigrants may have a space of their own, if they so wished. If they did not so wish, they were welcomed to Novus Mundus with open arms. The SUS was one of the few places on secondworld where capitalism was still considered a viable social and economic construct. Their obsession with gold and oil persisted.

The Southern Union States still had corporal punishment in place. Michael had seen a documentary on this on the 'boob-tube', and the more Victor spoke the more Michael was convinced Victor had seen the same documentary.

Lethal injection was the primary method on world-one, so this was the method adopted by most other secondworld counties with capital punishment. SUS favoured the rifleman.

The SUS all agreed that a second trial was futile, despite the evidence to the contrary.

Execution facilities were set up on the same sites as those located on world-one. Where possible advance information was sought on potential timeframes for any prisoners on death row but this was, principally, not forthcoming.
The facilities were monitored throughout the day and anyone coming in through this route was quickly dispatched again and sent on their way. SUS were not finessed. They had a guard in place at the location with a rifle, and orders to shoot any that materialised in the marked off area. This was a thankless task and given the infrequency of world-one executions you might forgive the allocated guard for taking a quick nap. This scenario played out at least once, where a guard had presumably been asleep at post. Someone had been executed on world-one, materialised on secondworld and went on to overpower and kill the attending guard. It was unclear if any guards of the world-one facility had been accidently killed on their entry to secondworld though this was a recognised risk.

"We are all guilty. All damaged souls. Where is the redemption? Where is the chance to live again?"

"And what are you going on about now?" interrupted Carol by way of announcement.
"Well good evening to you too, young lady." Victor beamed. "Michael and I were merely attempting a civilised conversation, safe in the knowledge that your arrival would disperse it."
"Just get me a drink Gandalf. You know that bird of yours is terrorising people out there." Carol responded. The falcon was not, in fact, 'terrorising people'; she was behaving impeccably, if not a little bit squawky.
"She is better behaved than most humans I will have you know." Victor declared before getting out of his seat and making his way to the bar. He would get Carol a brandy and she would be glad of it.
"Get me a cider!" Carol called after him.
He would get Carol a cider.

Her "So, what have you been you to then bub?"
Him "Not much, not with the rain."
Her "Yeah; pretty heavy earlier, beautiful now though."
Him "One of these days you're going to upset him you know."
Her "Ah, he loves me really. And I'm very fond of him too."
Him "You don't act like it."
Her "He's a miserable old sod, but he grows on you…. like gangrene."

Victor returned from the bar and took his seat, placing a drink before Carol.

"Thank you very much Victor." Said Victor.
"That's OK." Responded Carol and took a drink from her glass. She smiled as broadly as she could.

Victor knew she was saying 'OK' rather than 'okay' but he tried not to let it irk him. The truth was he enjoyed her company and spending time in the presence of the playful nature of this young woman.

The three chatted, and joked, and drank. Victor would pop out for a smoke every now and again.

A natural lull in the conversation presented itself, and Carol used this opportunity to, once again, confront Victor. She was partly trying to get another rise out of him, for her entertainment and the entertainment of others; but a greater part of her was genuinely interested in his response.

"Why are you always so hot under the collar anyways? Always something with you, isn't it?" said Carol.
"Yes. There is 'always something with me'. That's as it should be! To quote Dylan Thomas, who paraphrased Deacon Blue; 'I do not go gentle into that good night!'" Victor took to his feet and raised his glass.
"He's off again!" reported Carol.
"Rage against the dying of the light. Rage against the machine. Rage." continued Victor, unperturbed "But we are soft, and pliable. Downtrodden; distracted. It is hard to keep fire in your belly when your

belly is full. Our targets are off sight. We focus on the wrong foe. Some have nothing but fire in their belly, their focus on injustice is exact, but they have no power to influence or control the narrative. They scream into the void. Their voices diluted."

"Are you feeling quite alright?" Carol enquired.

Victor smiled and retook his seat. "Just a bit of theatrics, but sentiment is true, nonetheless. We need to remember to be good people. Above all else. Just be good and kind."

Carol did not ridicule him for this statement.

The night flowed and so did the drink, and as the night wore on Victor became more solemn, more melancholy.

Carol stopped for a few more drinks then said her goodbyes and made her way home. Michael would soon follow but wanted to make sure Victor was okay first. Victor had splintered off from the pair when he went outside for a smoke and was now chewing the ears off one of the members of the Middle Kingdom Traditionists.

"Bloody do-gooders!" "'Bloody do-gooders?' Going around, doing good. Have you listened to yourself?" There was no malice in his voice. Cheerful, but wrapped in sadness, with only the hint of a mocking tone. The verbal equivalent of a nudge to the elbow.

There seemed to be a particular sadness about some of his narration tonight. When Victor eventually took to his seat back next to Michael he confided in him. "I just want to remind people that the world we were born into on world-one was a nonsense. If you thought about it; I mean, really thought about it. But people never got the chance to think about it, did they? Here it is different, we can live a different life. It is not without its absurdities, but it is a life worth living. It is also delicate. We need to replicate the buildings on world-one but we should never revert to the ideology." And with that he closed his eyes. Michael paused for a moment and held his own breath. How long did Victor say he had left again? The eruption of snoring brought a sigh of relief from Michael.

New York crow

Declan Treanor

He wished he could remember the name of the artist, but the piece stuck with him. He had been to New York a few times over the years, he had friends there and so every now and again would pop over. At the time flights were relatively cheap, and he was young. He did the usual sight-seeing stuff but mostly went there to go to the bars and clubs. On one of these trips, he had visited the Guggenheim. He was not a philistine, nor was he a lovey. He thought he held an appropriate level of appreciation for the art that was presented to him and was willing to remain open to new experiences. The memory came to him both vivid and vague at the same time.

As he entered one of the rooms in the gallery, he became aware of an image on the far end wall. It appeared to be a couple of silhouettes, two busts. As he followed the natural path of the room he could see that the image was being projected on to the wall, rather than a painting or stencil. He walked closer. There was a single light source which cast the shadow. A male and a female; the male with a bird on their head; a crow. Tracking back, Michael could see that the shadow was cast by two spherical masses placed in the centre of the room. On closer examination the spheres revealed themselves to be two large masses of contorted taxidermy. Rats and voles. Carrion crows. Fish. Beautiful and bleak. He had spent longer than he should have done examining the animals.

Chris Cook

Waking up at 4 a.m. was just how Chris Cook operated. Her body didn't know anything else. It was as if her internal clock had been synchronized to the pre-dawn hours, a rhythm that pulsed through her veins. Her body was programmed to it, through habit, though given that this was a new body it must have been buried somewhere deep within her psyche. Chris was a baker. She was well aware of nominative determinism and could see in retrospect the path that led to her chosen career.

When she arrived in secondworld she decided she enjoyed being a baker and would continue to do so. This revelation came as somewhat of a surprise to Chris. Prior to her death she had considered baking as something that she had 'fallen into' or something of a 'stop gap' until she found a better job.

Her journey in the world of baking had its roots in a production setting. The hum of industrial mixers, the rhythmic thump of dough being kneaded, and the warmth of ovens working their magic—weaved together to form the symphony of a bustling bakery. Chris honed her skills in this environment, learning the alchemy of turning humble ingredients into the staff of life.

In the latter years of her career, a shift occurred. The transition from the production line to a more nuanced and artistic approach marked a new chapter in Chris's baking odyssey. The loaves became more than just sustenance; they transformed into expressions of creativity and craftsmanship.

As she delved into the intricacies of artisanal baking, Chris discovered a profound connection between her craft and the essence of her being. The early mornings, once driven by the need for efficiency, now carried a meditative quality—a sacred ritual where passion and precision intertwined.

In the quiet moments before the world awoke, Chris Cook, the baker, found solace in the alchemy of creation. A life filled with the tantalizing aromas of rising dough, the visual delights of golden crusts, and the thudding sound made by tapping the base of a loaf baked to perfection. The loaves, proofed and ready, bore witness to a journey that transcended the mere act of making bread; it was a life, richly kneaded and baked to precision. In these reflective moments she would consider, from time to time, what would have become of her if she had continued dealing drugs.

On her death, the connections of her hometown were no longer binding, so Chris found somewhere not too far that was in need of a baker, but also that she could picture herself in. This not so far place was Nesfield-upon-Hean. She felt it was of value to the community, and she was happy being part of that community.

Chris was allocated her accommodation, as everyone was, but she also petitioned for additional premises for the bakery. This was granted. If it had not been granted, she would have done what most did, set up a stall. Nobody could stop you from doing that. To be honest, nobody could have stopped her if she wanted to set up in the building without permission, it was just easier to get the forms. With the forms came support, and the community rallied round to help Chris with the set up. They all baked, but they were looking forward to having an actual bakery.

This was a morning like any other morning. Chris was up before most and making her way to the bakery. She felt safe here. Most people felt safe here, but Chris was used to hard streets and dark tunnels. She strode her normal route with confidence. She made her way down to the canal which served as a cut through.
As she rounded the corner something made her slow her pace.
In the inky black waters of the canal something was floating. She stopped dead and squinted at the object. She could not make out what it was. She forced her eyes away from the mass so that she could quickly assess the area. She could not see any signs of immediate danger, so Chris continued her journey, though at a very much reduced pace and her eyes firmly fixed on the object. She told herself 'I'm gonna laugh about this later' but was less than confident with the thought.

As she got closer the clump became more defined. Foreboding inched up her spine and crawled into her mind. 'Was it a body?' she asked herself the question though thought she already knew the answer. Her pace quickened towards it. 'It was, it was a person.' She ran to the side of the canal. Lying down on her stomach she reached out to the form.
Nowhere near.
Chris looked about her for something to aid with the recovery, then thought better of it. She jumped in. It came as a shock to Chris to discover that canals were not as shallow as she thought. She pawed at the side and managed to grasp hold of the bank. As she quickly composed herself she refocused on her mission.
Chris grabbed hold of the arm of the other person and heaved herself up on to the towpath. Rolling on to her side Chris kept hold of the person's arm. She pulled the body, still floating face down, closer to the bank, then grunted with effort as she pulled and grappled the body on to dry land. As Chris came face-to-face with the woman for the first time, the very faint glimmer of hope that she may be able to revive her, vanished. The woman's face was grey and puffy.
'She must have tripped and fallen in.' Chris thought absent-mindedly to herself. 'Poor old dear.'

Chris looked up and down the canal. It was still too early, no signs of life. She decided she would have to leave the body unattended while she went to get some help. The bakery would have to wait today.

Declan Treanor

The body

Jackie had heard about the body being found through village gossip rather than any official reporting route. By the time she had arrived on the scene the body and any witnesses had long gone. Jackie heard that it was Chris Cook who had pulled the body from the canal, she had also heard that the body was Florance but was dismissing this from her mind until she had confirmed this herself. Jackie went from the canal to Cook's bakery, but a sign in the window informed her that the shop was closed for the day 'due to unforeseen circumstances.' Jackie finally tracked Cook down at home.

The kettle was boiled, pastries were plated, the tea brewed and eventually poured. Only then was the interview conducted. Jackie and Chris were on nodding terms with each other and were aware of each other in the way that most of the village were aware of Jackie and Chris due to their respective roles. The interview was informal, as most things on secondworld were.

Jackie started. "Firstly, are you okay? It must have been quite a shock."

"No, I'm fine. Really." Chris replied "Not like I aint seen a dead body before... I used to be one!"

Jackie gave Chris a look that Chris either did not interpret or chose to ignore. "So, what happened then?" Jackie resumed. Chris told her about finding the body and going to get help, she then backtracked to briefly describe her routine that morning before finding Florence. "So, after you got the body out?" Jackie was eager to find out where the body was now but was also happy to hear how things progressed chronologically.

"Well, we couldn't leave poor old Florence on the ground, could we? It was too late for her, and people would be getting up, so we moved her. Put her in the GP."

"And she's still there now?" Jackie enquired.

"As far as I know." The GP surgery was not used on a regular basis, just now and again, usually to treat accidents. Jackie went over a few more details before asking if Chris would be willing to accompany her to formally identify the body. Chris was happy to do this though there seemed little doubt who it was. Before they left the apartment Jackie made it clear to Chris that she should have informed the police about the body, and that moving it could be construed as tampering with evidence. Chris apologised for her actions and promised not to do it again.

Teeth

He stuttered awake. Flickered into being. The room was sun warmed. Images still remained of his dream. Vivid, yet fractured. He was aware that this was not the first time he had awoke this morning. The first one didn't stick. He wanted to return to slumber. Return to the dreamworld he had created. A world of patterns and peril. He wanted to rewrite the ending. To give his fellow self the tools to fight and win. He was a child. He was at school again, hiding in the toilets, in a cubicle. He could hear the monster on the other side. Breathing heavily, drawing in the aroma of his prey. He could sense the longing, the desire to devour. He could hear the fangs foaming, drool and blood; he could smell the rictus grin. He could taste the wolfen matted hide. 'Oh grandma, what big eyes you have'. The slow, laboured padding of feet stopped. Stopped outside the cubicle he was in. His feet stood on the toilet bowl to avoid immediate detection. He held his breath. The latch opened by itself, and the door creaked open. An instant before the monster lunged, a change of perspective. He dove toward himself with a lust for blood.

The Garden Hermit

The main tavern in Nesfield-upon-Hean was the 'Garden Hermit'. It was, in fact, the only tavern. There were tap rooms and bar rooms, and bars in living rooms, but the Green Hermit was the only authentic pub. The landlady, Mary, was just coming up to her final year and had already nominated her successor. This had been done correctly and following due process. The Bureau had been notified and the candidate proposed. No other nominations had been put forward, but a ballot still needed to be held. This was done for a reason that no one quite remembered, but it was an excuse to get the town together and put some bunting up. In Nesfield-upon-Hean the bunting was rarely down. The past the post number was 20% of populus. 461 was the number of favourable ballots needed for Simon to take over from Mary. Simon was well liked and did this with ease.

Victor was, of course, a regular.

The name of the pub derived from the late, great, William Eldridge. He was a prominent figure in the development of secondworld which he did from his base of Nesfield-upon-Hean.

He was one of the figureheads involved in developing the structure of how the Kingdom would operate, and the establishment of safeguards to prevent this structure being exploited.

Prior to his death he had also been quite a character.

William had spent time in the service of the Habsburg's, a well-to-do couple and 27th in line to the Austrian throne. The Habsburgs longed to be part of the Victorian society. They had adopted the modern craze of housing a hermit on their grounds. This was quite the status symbol of the time, and a talking point of all Hasburg Manors guests.

William was a hermit by profession, and profession only. He played the role well and was well paid for this service. He had the ability to look melancholy but furtive in quick succession. William would make sure that he was seen by members of the household and their guests roaming the grounds, sometimes as if lost in thought, sometimes foraging, and at other times acting in quite a bizarre fashion altogether, involved in some mysterious task that those who observed would never fathom. William, dressed in his ragged clothes and unwashed, would engross himself in the given activity until he was sure that he had his audience captivated, at that point he would feign a realisation that he was being watched and scarper into the nearest hedgerow or thicket.

Sometimes, he would not been seen for days, but whenever there was a big social event at the house. The periods of absence only added to the mystery of the man. In reality, William had quite the life outside of his hermitry.

He had a modest but clean residence on the grounds and a further flat in Chelsea. At times he socialised with London elite. Some of these same people could be found, at one time or another, gawping at him in his other role as a hermit. They would never have guessed. He had played cricket for Kent at one stage and even played against the great W. G. Grace. William could often be found having luncheon at the Savoy.

As the years passed, he became more reclusive. To the Manor House at least. He met a girl. This led to a difficult conversation with his employer. "What good is a hermit that is never there?" the master of the house complained.

They agreed on at least four sightings a week with one of those demonstrating an extremely bizarre behaviour; William would be available for all social events at the Manor if booked in advance.

The arrangement continued in this way until his untimely death. Vicent had been intoxicated and had been choked to death by his shirt collar. This was not an uncommon occurrence. In fact, the type of collar was nicknamed the 'Father Killer' for that very reason.

His death brought new sobriety to the man. He was still vibrant and passionate, but he put aside most of his follies and dedicated himself to the evolution of society. And did this well.

The 'Middle Kingdom Traditionalists' met here weekly on a Thursday and felt a deep affinity with William Eldridge. Though an outside observer would struggle with the comparison.

23AM

Declan Treanor

The Middle Kingdom Traditionalists

The Middle Kingdom Traditionalists were as near to a political opposition organisation as was allowed. They were classed as a sect, and held no office, and their modus was one of petition. The sects were spread throughout the Kingdom and organised through a central hub. Each of the sects would hold a meeting, at least weekly, to discuss the enjoyment of life, and how this could be curtailed. From the outsider this would seem to be all that was done. Meeting after meeting. The standing agenda included social housing, immigration, and any other business. The social housing discussion usually centred around some of the group lamenting the loss of their expansive home before begrudgingly admitting that it was probably too big to manage without help. The discussion around immigration involved someone reporting that they had heard there was soon to be a mass migration from a country. The location and reason for mass exodus changed, but the destination was always the hallowed ground of the Kingdom. This topic would peter out as the group knew in their hearts that if this mass migration ever happened, which up to now had not, that there would be enough resources to manage and that welcoming these people would be the right thing to do. This was seldom vocalised and never minuted. The last item was where the real action happened. This contained all manner of delightful topics from loud letterboxes to unsightly goats.

The minutes of each meeting would be viewed by the hub and any outcomes, actions, or requests would be forwarded to the Bureau including deadlines for entry. These deadlines were never met, the petition seldom reviewed. In general, it tended to be the same requests with one or two digressions.

Every once and a while the petition would find its way to the desk of someone who felt obligated to reply. A reply was sent that the board of such-and-such was taking these matters into consideration. Whenever one of these letters was received it meant that they could not open their meeting with the standard vitriolic speech condemning the lack of response. Sometimes if a reply was received it may be put to the side until the following meeting, especially if the speech for that week had already been written. The reply would eventually be read out, then the focus would be on why the issues had not yet been addressed. Sometimes a more comprehensive reply would be received. This would require further dissection and multiple emergency meetings, though ultimately the natural order of things would come to balance, and the committee would revert to type.

These societies, though pervasive, were ultimately harmless. A toothless echo of a once powerful entity. A castrated Office. A drawn-out death rattle manifested by grumblings in a church hall. A slow demise, minuted and documented to be filed and forgotten. A comfort blanket for those that did not wish for change. Most of the members did not believe in the cause they just wanted to meet up and have cake.

There was a certain nostalgia for world-one. This was very much like any other kind of nostalgia. You recall the good things, and only wish for its return as you know it is impossible. If you really had the chance to swap what was current with what was past, with all of the downsides, with all of the restrictions, would you make the trade?

"Oooo, remember Planet of the Apes ice-cream? You got a free mask, didn't you?" The miners strike and football hooliganism aside.

Nobody wanted the phones back. The convenience was sacrificed for the renewed freedoms. No longer shackled to the device that demanded constant attention. They could pretend they did, but these arguments weren't very convincing.

Processed foods were desired though. "I can't remember the last time I ate something that wasn't artisan!" they would bemoan. A whole afternoon could be spent talking about 'Turkey Twizzlers'. People tried to make their own but they always turned out tasting like actual food.

Another lorded pastime was to gather the newest cohorts and quiz them about world-one. You were considered very good company if you were able to describe with detail how everything on world-one was 'going down the pan.'

Unrequited. A love affair with a time and place that was not reciprocated.

Declan Treanor

Today, however, proceedings did not hold their usual form. Today was a solemn occasion. Since last they met, they had heard of the untimely demise of one of their own. A member of the Middle Kingdom Traditionists had been taken before her time. The meeting was being held in the Garden Hermit as the group had been barred from the village hall for unseemly behaviour, when one of the members had become overly excited during a debate and damaged a hanging basket on his exit.

"I would like to bring the meeting to order, please," stated Alfred, the meeting chair. He waited for those rearranging themselves to finish their arrangements. "If I may, I would like to break from protocol to firstly acknowledge the passing of our fellow member, and friend, Florence Ward." A dignified silence was observed before business resumed as normal.

Maureen enquired as to whether the 'break from protocol' should be included in the minutes and was informed that it should.

Market

He knew he knew him from somewhere, but where? This Swiss-cheese memory of his was becoming a bind. "Hello, have we met before?"

"No, I don't think so." He had a handsome smile. The smile was only held briefly. Still handsome though. Michael thought he saw a flicker of recognition.

"Are you sure we haven't met; you look very familiar?"

"No, sorry." The reply was curt and was meant to curtail any further exploration of the topic.

"It's just that..." Michael was cut off.

"I'm sorry, I can't help you." The man strode off.

'That was odd.' He would not have considered it odd before he died. 'That was more of a world-one interaction.' Michael thought to himself. Ever since he had arrived on secondworld Michael had found that people were always happy to engage, that above all people were polite and kind, and thoughtful. 'Perhaps the guy hadn't been here that long. Perhaps he thought I was coming on to him? Was I? It did sound like a line, but he was sure he had met the guy before. That he knew him from world-one. '

Michael turned around to find Victor standing directly behind him. "Jesus, you scared the life outa me."

"That was the general idea." Replied Victor.

The Twin

Henry was a twin. His brother, also a twin, was still on world-one. If truth be known Henry's name was not Henry. It was Martin.

The twin boys were called Henry and Martin. They were named and christened as such. At some point without ceremony, they swapped names. Henry and Martin would never know this. Their parents had just lost track one day. They knew one was Henry and one was Martin but at some point the consensus had altered. As they grew older you could easily tell them apart but by that stage it was too late. The names had stuck. If you name something incorrectly for a long enough period, it becomes that thing. The name changes. This is true. But it must be recognised that the baby that was Christened Henry was now called Martin, and the baby that was christened Martin was the person people called Henry. All their documentation stated this was not the case, all apart from the birth certificates. Nobody would ever know this fact. The universe knew but cared little.

Henry had been visiting Catney that day to barter for some orange wine. There was nothing unusual about that, he often spent his time travelling to nearby villages and towns through the canal system. He had a push barge. This was a narrowboat to all intents and purposes, built by Henry but punted down the canal, instead of any kind of engine. It was much lighter but surprisingly sturdy.

As he attended the market, a market that he had attended many times before, a feeling of unease came upon him. He could not explain it. He became vaguely aware that someone was talking to him. He provided answers to the male, but his mind was hazy, cluttered. He felt the overwhelming need to get back to his boat, back to safety of the water. The bustling marketplace was not conducive to whatever the hell was going on. He manoeuvred himself away from the main throng and found a wall to lean against. He steeled himself and did a quick assessment. He was 'okay'. Was he okay? Yes, he was okay. He felt the muscle returning to his legs and his cerebral fluid had begun the process of slowing its eddying. Should he try to get some help. No, he would just return to the boat, have a green tea and then be on his way. Strike that, he thought, I will get going and brew the tea on the go. He could not understand why it was important that he left this place but knew with certainty that he would not feel better until he had some miles between him and Catney. The neanderthal part of his brain had awoken. The cave man's instinct said to run.

Not again

As Chris rounded the corner, she became aware of a dark patch in the already inky back water of the canal. There was something floating? No, it was her mind playing tricks with her. She hesitantly edged closer. Chris stopped and looked around her. Not the slightest shift, all was still. Even the birdsong in its infancy did not betray its composer's location through movement. Chris continued on her path. It quickly became clear that history was repeating itself. "Not again" Chris muttered to herself "I've gotta find a different route to work."

-

The banging on the door woke Jackie from her slumber. Dragging her body from the bedcovers her feet fumbling beneath her, she pulled a t-shirt over her head then stepped clumsily into some jogging bottoms. She neither lit a lamp nor displayed a hint of caution when she swung open the door. When Jackie's sleep filled eyes adjusted to the predawn light, the best she could muster was to announce her guest. "Cook!" she said.

"Thought I'd better come tell ya, I've found another body....by the canal."

Jackie blinked a few times. "I'll get some shoes." was the eventual reply. Jackie left the door ajar and went to the bedroom. A moment later she reappeared hopping as she put on her second trainer.

-

It was only a short distance from Jackie's flat to the location of the second body. "I remembered what you said about not moving the body, you know, from last time." They had both broken into a slight jog. Chris continued "A bloke this time, I think. Don't think I could have dragged him out on my own, even if I thought it worthwhile. Lump of a thing. Definitely dead though. Far as I could see." They reached the canal and stood for a moment to observe the floating figure. "See, it's a bloke this time."

Jackie, still silent, looked around the immediate vicinity. She was looking for a discarded weapon or a blood splatter, or anything that might be out of place. No such luck. She turned to Chris "Do you think you could give me a hand getting them out? If you don't fancy it, I can get someone else."

Chris rolled up her sleeves as she knelt down. "I did the last one, didn't I?" She stretched out towards the body but could not reach.

Jackie found a stray branch and though it was not overly thick it held enough strength to start the body drifting toward the bank. When Chris had a firm hold of one of the arms Jackie discarded the stick and grabbed the other arm. Between them they were able to scramble the corpse onto the towpath. They tried as best they could not to damage the remains any further but if truth be known, some of the abrasions to the face and arms had been done postmortem.

Post-Jackie and Chris.

Placing him supine both Jackie and Chris recognised the man. It would have been more surprising if they had not. Everyone knew everyone.

"That's one of the barge blokes. Isn't it?" Jackie offered.

"Yeah. Comes in the bakery the odd time. Whatisname? He spends the summer here then heads back north." They stood over the body. His face was reddened and starting to bloat though still recognisable, some blackening was apparent around the nose, mouth and eyes, swollen shut.

"Odd innit?" Chris waited for a response. When none was forthcoming, she pitched again. "Two bodies, same place. Strange."

If Cook was fishing for information, Jackie thought, she had come to the wrong place. Jackie did not have a clue what was going on. On world-one there would be discussions around possible causes, probable causes, potential suspects and hidden motives. There would have been others to have the discussions with. "You didn't do it did you?" Jackie eyed her one and only suspect to look for signs of gilt or nervousness.

"Why would I?" the answer was higher pitched than Jackie would have liked. Jackie waited.

"No. I did not kill either of 'em." Chris' tone had returned to type.

As there was no one else to discuss this with, Jackie thought, she may as well discuss it with Cook, and now that she had ruled her out of her enquiries… "So, coincidence?"

Chris looked at Jackie, then back at the body. "I don't really believe in 'em."

"Me neither." Jackie retorted as she knelt by the body. She did, of course, believe in coincidences. Bumping into someone you know when on holiday, wearing the same top as a friend, sharing a birthday with someone; these were coincidences. What Jackie meant was that she didn't think these deaths were coincidental. She thought that there was more to it. To have articulated this would not have sounded as snappy. She was pleased with her quip.

Jackie took a closer look at the face. It was difficult to know what she was looking for. Something out of the ordinary she guessed. Usually forensics did all this. She could recall something about if someone was found face down in water that meant they drowned but could not recall if that came from work or from a crime drama. If that were the case, would it rule out murder? She was less than confident so put the thought out of her mind.

The man's gnarled hands were wrinkled to the point where the upper layer of skin was detaching itself. Jackie winced inwardly and was about to stand back up when she noticed a thin leather bracelet. She carefully edged this away from his cuff so that it was more in view. "Cook. Do you know what this is?"

Chris lent forward to examine the bracelet closer whilst trying to ignore his ravaged hand. "Just a bracelet, isn't it?"

Jackie stood up and dusted her knees. "Florence had one just like it."

Innocent again

The body was moved to the local GP surgery once Jackie had enlisted some more volunteers. The surgery was just a replica husk of its world-one counterpart, but it was suited to this purpose. Jackie had managed to remove Henry's clothing and examine the body further. There were abrasions which would have been consistent with falling in a canal, floating along a canal and being dragged out of a canal. There was, however, a puncture wound in the back of the neck which appeared to be quite deep. Jackie having no resources to explore this further had to rely on her gut. 'Foul play.' She concluded. She thought she had better take this to Innocent. He would not do anything, and it was not procedure, there was no procedure, but she thought it best that he knew.

When she eventually got through the door, Innocent was predictably dismissive. "What could possibly connect these two people?" he asked. "Apart from the bracelet?" Jackie countered "and where the bodies were found?" she continued before Innocent could interrupt "and the mark on his neck? Did Florence have one too?"
"We will never know about Florence, and we cannot be sure that his mark was not done after he fell in the canal. You admit you cannot be sure how deep it is."
"I was thinking about sticking a skewer down there." Jackie had thought of that on the way over.
"I will not have the body of a resident of Nesfield-upon-Hean desecrated without reason." Innocent retorted.
"Fair point." He was not a resident, but Jackie was not here to argue. For once she had work to do. "I'll just ask around a bit, see if anyone saw anything. Same as we did with Florence. He was probably out drinking and fell in."
Innocent was not entirely stupid; he knew that whatever he chose to say would have little or no impact on the preceding actions of Jackie Taylor. He looked her squarely in the eye. "We just don't want to create hysteria Jackie. Do what needs to be done."
And with that she dismissed herself.

The conversation held with Innocent was not a total fabrication. 'I'll just ask around a bit, see if anyone saw anything. Same as we did with Florence.' What else could she do? There was only her. It was a start at least. What connected these two? Was there a connection? She hadn't looked at Florence's house last time. 'Sloppy. Very secondworld.' She thought. Florance had already been cremated, but it would be easy enough to find out if anyone had been given her personal effects. She would confirm there was a second bracelet, look at both their residents, and then go knocking door-to-door. She wondered if Cook would like to join her.

An Investigation

Getting hold of Florence's personal effects was easy enough. These had been given to the chair of the Middle Kingdom Traditionalists. He seemed quite keen to be shot of them, and Jackie thought he probably had very little use for them. There was a handkerchief, a necklace made of twine and wooden beads, and the leather bracelet. The bracelet was indeed identical to the one that the boatman had worn. Jackie had asked whether any purse or coins had been retrieved from the body. The chairman appeared quite flustered when responding to this, but she believed him when he said that nothing else had been passed to him. Jackie assured him that it was not an accusation, it just struck her as odd that she did not have anything on her. And where was her door key?

Jackie had to admit to herself that lots of people on secondworld went about their lives never carrying money, or even thinking about it, but she had always found that the older generation liked to have something on them, just in case. People carried their housekey though. Everyone did, surely?

Jackie and Chris had agreed to meet outside Florence's apartment, and then carry on to the boat following. "Morning Cook." Jackie said and held up her crowbar in greeting.

"Morning Jackie. I wish you would call me Chris though." Chris replied. She had been thinking this for some time but only now felt comfortable enough to address it.

"Not a chance, Cook." Came the immediate reply. "Shall we?" Jackie led the way up to the apartment. When she got to the front door she tried the handle. She was not expecting it to be unlocked but did not want to start crowbarring open a door without first entertaining the option.

It opened.

"Well, what do ya know?" Jackie exclaimed.

She tentatively entered the apartment closely followed by Chris.

"So, what are we looking for?" Chris asked.

"Clues." Jackie replied.

"So, what would be classed as a clue then?" Chris continued. She thought she would know one when she saw one but did not want to miss something that Jackie may have deemed obvious.

"Well, for starters the door was unlocked. Does she normally go out and leave the door unlocked?" Jackie replied. She scanned the apartment. It was like any other in the village with only the slightest of differences made by the addition of gaudy soft furnishings. It looked as though it was usually kept tidy, and was only betrayed now by a cold, half-drunk cup of tea that sat next a book and a completely burnt-out wick lantern. It was as if the room had been abruptly vacated.

"A cup of tea, unfinished; and a wick lantern, burned-out." Jackie gestured towards the items with her crowbar as she named them. "It doesn't look like there was a struggle here, but it certainly looks like she left in a hurry."

"Or maybe she just thought she was coming back." Chris added.

Cook had made a very good point. Jackie acknowledged this by the use of silence.

It was evident that no one had been in. "Didn't anyone come back to get clothes for the cremation?" Jackie asked.

"I think they just kept her in the clothes she was found in. They had dried out by then." Chris replied.

Slightly disrespectful, Jackie thought but was grateful they didn't; her potential crime scene was left untouched.

Jackie continued to take in the room, walking a circuit of it. There was a bookcase, crammed with books of all types, though the dominating topic appeared to be platypuses. The far end of the bookcase was occupied by a gramophone. The stylus rested on the vinyl, though the hand cranked turntable had long since ceased its rotations. Jackie placed her crowbar on the fireplace. She removed the needle from the record and read the label; 'Schubert's Finished Symphony'.

There was a straw hat on the kitchen worktop. Was this a spare? She could not remember seeing Florence without her hat. Could this be a line of enquiry? She made a mental note. Then, remembering that she often forgot things, she took out her pad and pen and made a physical note.

"Do you ever remember seeing Florence without her hat?" Jackie asked as she jotted things down in her book.
Chris thought for a while before answering. "No, I don't think I have."
"And you didn't find one at the canal?" Jackie continued.
"No, nothing." Chris was currently looking at the good quality picture of a person that was not Florence's husband. She picked it up. "Do you think this was her husband?" She held up the picture.

Jackie looked over. "Probably." Jackie went over to the window. She could see the canal below and could almost see the very spot where Florence had been found. Jackie spent a bit more time looking in boxes and drawers but really didn't turn up much. In the bedroom she came across the crude drawing of Leonard and wondered who it might be.

On Florence's dresser was a purse with some coins inside; Jackie also made a note of this in her book. Under her bed was a box full of unopened letters. They looked old. Most likely letters from her husband, Jackie thought, but why were they unopened? Jackie contemplated whether or not she should open one to confirm her suspicion. She took the first one on the pile and broke the seal. It was indeed from Florence's husband. Jackie did not read much of it, only enough to confirm that they held no relevance. The envelope also included a photograph of the man. He looked nothing like the picture in the lounge.

The flat would be cleared out soon. Letters, pictures and other personal items would go into storage for future relatives, but everything else would be cleaned or, if damaged, replaced. Another soul to occupy the space for an absolute maximum of 23-years.

What had they established? Jackie went over what she felt were the key points in her mind while making bullet points in her notepad.

- FW left the apartment suddenly
- cold tea, candle, record-player, no key, no money, no hat (but did have coat)
- She might have thought she was coming back/would only be a while???
- She could see the canal from her flat
- No signs of a struggle in the flat
- get milk on way home

Jackie decided to go and have a look at the barge. This room could not tell her anything more. She picked up her crowbar and closed the door, leaving the room, more-or-less, as she had found it.

-

As they walked along the canal toward where the twin's boat was now moored, Jackie scanned the area for any further evidence, or anything out of place. She had already done this but thought it wouldn't hurt to do it again. She also directed Cook to do the same. 'Two heads, and all that.'

As she walked and scanned, she thought about what Innocent had said; 'We just don't want to create hysteria Jackie. Do what needs to be done.' If he had forbade Jackie to look into these deaths, she would have anyway. If he had stripped her title, she would have acted the same. Who was going to stop her? There were no other police and Innocent was not the type to get his own hands dirty.

He was, however, happy for her hands to get dirty. 'Do what needs to be done.' He just wanted this issue to go away. Back to the quiet life. Was that so bad? What was the alternative? What would Innocent do if she forced the matter? She was not worried about the consequences imposed on her. No, she was tough and resourceful. But she had the feeling there was a Machiavellian side to Innocent; a side that was currently docile, happy to remain dormant and placid. A well-fed shark. Not a threat unless aroused by the smell of blood.

-

They had arrived at the location of the houseboat. Again, the crowbar was surplus to requirements, so Jackie laid this on the towpath.

After the discovery of the body, the barge had been found adrift further down the canal. It was retrieved using a boathook and a big leap, and had been moored once more to its original location. The bargepole had been found floating nearby, tangled in some brush.

"Let me go on first." Said Jackie as she stepped onto the craft. She wanted to check out a theory. If the boat was adrift and the body was found in the canal it stood to reason that whatever happened, happened when he was driving, sailing, punting? In motion.

Jackie stood on the deck. Though there was no engine there was a tiller, and a platform, to the rear of the boat. The floor of this platform was stained. Jackie knelt down and touched the dark tacky blotch. When she removed her fingers, they were reddened. "Blood." Jackie announced.

She was pretty sure that's what it was. There were no labs set up for this, no procedural requirements. She thought that, if needed, she could request this from the Bureau, but was it needed? Not at this stage. And what would it prove anyway? That he hit his head somehow?

She thought it odd they were found in the same place but reasoned that Cook had found them in the basin, just before the turn. If they had been dumped in any part of the stretch of this part of the canal, it would be likely that the lock would draw them down to settle there. The only reason the barge had not done the same was due to its size.

"Okay Cook, you can come on." Jackie told Chris before opening the hatch to the cabin and disappearing inside. Jackie found a sink and washed off the remnants of the twin from her fingers.

The narrowboat was narrow.

Jackie navigated the space as best she could with Cook.

Brief imaginings of a life on the water sparked in Jackie's mind. She could travel. Tour the country. This boat was going spare. Maybe. She would solve the case first.

"Why would you have a picture of yourself?" Chris offered. She mistakenly thought it was a picture of Henry. It was.

Chris idly poked around the space available to her, opening and closing drawers. "Why are we doing this blind? Surely the Bureau would have some details on these pair?"

This is why she had brought Cook. There was not much linking them in this world, but what about the previous one? What clues did the Bureau hold? She would write up a request for their files tonight and put it in the post. They would have it by tomorrow afternoon. It would probably take a bit of time, not because anyone was trying to be obstructive, it was just a processing issue.

"I've already requested their files. It just takes a while." Jackie lied, not for herself, but so that Cook could maintain her faith in the capabilities of the police force. At least that is what she told herself, which was fair. One lie for Cook, one lie for Jackie.

There were pots and pans, and plates and cups; beds that folded down and tables that folded up; fishing lines and fishing lures; jumpers, waders, filters, buckets and ropes.

The inside of the boat gave them nothing. Nothing that held interest. Nothing that made things any clearer. At least she had confirmed that the boatman had met his end whilst at the tiller. In her mind he had been killed. Someone had got onto the boat and stabbed him in the back of the neck. Was he facing him? Did he struggle? Who knows?

She would get up early and knock doors.

Did she need some more heroin? No, she had some actual work to do. She would get to bed early. Early to bed, early to rise.

23AM

Jackie at been somewhat introverted on the walk down to the barge; lost in her own thoughts. Chris had respected this.

Chris didn't for the life of her think that Jackie had requested the files from the Bureau but was happy that she may have been some help today.

Dog

Through the grapevine Michael had heard that someone had a basset hound they needed to home. The dog had materialised in the home of someone that only had a few months left. Firstly, they thought that it might be unfair on the dog if they kept it, as it would lose another owner in a relatively short period of time. They also had a suspicion that saying goodbye to a dog they had grown to love may make their second-death infinitely more painful.

When Michael met the dog, he was immediately smitten. He knew this would be the case. His new companion.

They walked home together. The dog waddling alongside its new owner on a makeshift lead. When they reached his apartment Michael created a bed for the dog using some cushions while the dog explored its new home.

The dog needed a name. 'Dog' seemed appropriate. This was partial homage to the TV show 'Columbo' and partially, so the animal wasn't confused. Whatever name he came up with would have been strange to the canine, but he was certain that he would have been referred to as 'Dog' from time to time.

Michael got Dog some scrags of raw meat and put them in the bowl that would be henceforth known as the dog bowl. He also set down some water.

After Dog had orientated himself both he and Michael went out to the village again. Michael managed to get hold of a lead that was a bit more fit-for-purpose and put in an order for a collar complete with nametag. Michael had already established himself firmly in this community, but the introduction of Dog cemented his position. He was happy here. Here was happy with him. He was happy with his dog. Here was happy with Dog.

The Kingdom position on dog poo was the same as everywhere else, get rid of it. If you were walking with your dog, you picked it up. Michael didn't mind that. He was used to it. It was strange that he didn't mind picking up his own dogs but retched at the thought of picking up another dog's poo. It was like babies, and their nappies he supposed. He remembered this one time his dog had a poo whilst off the lead in a park, they were some distance away. He walked over to the spot and looked around. He picked up what he thought was his dogs mess. When he gripped it, using the hand in bag technique, it was cold. The horror! He still picked it up, but he was disgusted.

The rule about picking up dog poo was obviously only relevant when you were with your dog. A lot of dogs on secondworld roamed free. Even the ones with owners would canter about ownerless when their owners were otherwise engaged. The social contract was that if you saw dog poo and you had a stick, you pushed the poo into a bush.

Dog and Michael spent the evening sitting watching the boob-tube. Michael watched, Dog slept and nuzzled into Michael on the sofa. Michael had a newfound evening habit of having a cheese and onion sandwich with a whiskey and water. The bread was white; the cheese, thick cut cheddar; the onion raw. Michael like to drink alcohol from the shabbiest glass he could find. It reminded him of the jazz basements he had once visited in Prague and tasted all the better for it. When preparing the sandwich this particular evening, Michael was reminded of the 'cheese tax' that all dogs extort. Those bloodshot eyes drilling into his soul until squares of cheese were shared. Michael was not daft though, he ate first, the dog ate after.

Before Michael retired, he reminded the dog where the dog bed was, and bid him goodnight. At some point during the early stages of sleep Michael became aware of Dog joining him in the human bed. Michael did little to discourage this.

door to door

Carol opened the door. "Good afternoon. I am police constable Jackie Taylor." Jackie, on saying this, held up the ID that hung around her neck. The ID was not standard. In truth, all she was given to commemorate her appointment was a coin which was stamped with the word 'police' on one side and 'non-transferable' on the other. Jackie had taken this coin to a Tanner she knew, and he had incorporated this into quite an impressive, and official looking, embossed lanyard. "You may have heard," Jackie continued "that there have been some recent second-deaths by the canal. Two, to be exact. Though not currently thought to be suspicious," she lied "we would appreciate any information you can offer that may help our enquiries."

Jackie had reeled off this opener eight times already today before breaking into a more natural conversation based on who the individual was. She felt she needed to initially establish the tone, 'set out her stall' so to speak. She wanted to make it clear that it was not a social call. This was a danger, as the seven people before this, Jackie had known well, and had indeed made social calls on them from time-to-time. "Hi, I don't think we've met," Jackie stuck out her hand "Jackie."

Carol shook her hand "Carol. Pleased to meet you. Do you want to come in?" Carol led the way into her double occupancy residence. This did not go unnoticed by Jackie.

Small talk ensued whilst Carol put on the kettle; though 'small talk' on secondworld usually consisted of 'Well, how did you die then?' and 'Are any of your family dead?' Through this Jackie got to learn about Carol's husband and her son still on world-one. There were some tears but despite or perhaps because of her hard exterior Jackie was very good at consoling people.

Jackie then moved on to the matter in hand. "So, do you remember where you were three days ago?" Most people, especially ones who were nowhere near their end time, didn't rely on days and dates and lost track pretty quickly. She retrieved a notebook and pencil from the side pocket of her trousers. "It would have been the day after your husband passed for the second time." Jackie tried to put this as delicately as she could.

"Oh, yeah. Right. Well, I was here then. I wasn't in a great state." She bowed her head as if ashamed by her grief.
"That's understandable." said Jackie softly. "Did you go out for anything? For a walk? To get food?" "I'm not even sure that I even ate that day, if I'm honest. I was in bed mostly. Not sleeping. Not really awake." Carol found it hard to access these memories again. It was still too raw. Jackie left a respectful pause and sipped her tea. She didn't really want the tea, she had already had six cups before she got to Carol's.
"Do you remember seeing anything, hearing anything?" Jackie stood up and looked out of the living room window, "You're right on top of the canal here and it would have been warm. I'm guessing you would have had your windows open?"
Without word Carol put down her cup of tea and went into her bedroom. Jackie was unsure whether to follow but repositioned herself so that she could see Carol through the open doorway. Carol was stood in the bedroom looking down at the canal, framed by a Juliet balcony. "There was something." Carol said, almost to herself. She turned to face Jackie. "Not that night, but another night. Maybe the second person. The man. I was asleep and something woke me up. I thought it was a scream at the time, but then talked myself out of it. I went to the balcony. Lads, messing about I thought." Carol was looking to her mind's eye, her brow furrowed. Jackie gave her space to think. "Sorry, it's no good. I just remember some figures. It was dark."
"Do you know what time it was?" Jackie chanced.
"No, sorry. I think I just went to the toilet and then back to bed." Carol replied.

Jackie fumbled in her other trouser pocket and produced a leather strap. "I don't suppose you recognise this?" she said and handed it over to Carol.
"What is it?" asked Carol as she turned it over in her hand.
"Not sure." Jackie replied not wanting to offer a guess herself.
"It looks kinda familiar but have no idea where from." Carol handed the item back to Jackie. "I'm sorry I couldn't be more help." Carol lamented.

"Not at all, thank you for your time." Jackie produced a card. "If you remember anything please give me a call. If I'm out, leave a message. I check them daily." And with that Jackie was gone.

Carol needed to get going, she was meeting Michael for dinner, but first she would sit for a moment and finish her tea. She was sure she had seen that strap before, but where?

Luca Rossi

There was a small restaurant in the village that Michael, in this short period, came to love, and frequented whenever possible. He had quickly established himself in the village as being quite handy, a trait leftover from his younger years. This allowed him to earn a few coins here and there, though the ability to pay was in no way a prerequisite to the help being given. The restaurant, if it could be referred to as such, had no reservations and no opening hours. If it was open, it was open. If it was shut, you kept on walking. Today it was open. Michael walked in, the puppy in tow. His presence was announced by a traditional shopkeepers' bell. A head popped out from the kitchen.

"Michael! Come in. Come, sit." The greeting was supplied by Luca Rossi. His surname was actually Ellis, but he decided to use his mother's maiden name for the restaurant. He held no grievance with his father nor wanted to disassociate himself with that part of his heritage, he just thought it sounded better and his dad agreed.

Luca had always wanted to be a restauranteur but without the funds it was a risky venture. A pipe dream which occupied the odd Sunday afternoon. From time-to-time he would revisit the project, looking at vacant venues on-line or typing up a business plan, but that was as far as it went. He had real bills to pay without conjuring the imagined expenditure of premises, and industrial cookers and whatever else was required. It was a major financial risk and he worried that if he chanced it, and it was not successful, he may never recover from it. His death allowed him to make the change.

He did not rush into it, however. Luca and his father, who was also dead, spent time travelling. They went to places that they had always wanted to see before it was too late. Now that it was, technically, 'too late' they went to see the replicant sight instead.

Christ the Redeemer; the Great Wall of China; the Fairy Chimneys of Cappadocia; the Great Pyramid of Khufu.

The pyramids were, for the most part, prefabricated. A latter addition. When the Pharaohs passed on to secondworld they found a less than subservient workforce and the whip and manacle were found lacking. New Gods were being worshiped with the old. Ptah was heralded as the God above Gods. The God of thought and creativity. The Pharaohs arrived to secondworld in poverty, not surrounded by all their worldly goods as they had planned and not enclosed in their tombs. Those that tried to regain their power were told where to go (but in hieroglyphics). After all this, there were pharaoh's who still considered themselves divine. Those that did not listen met with the Assessors of Ma'at and underwent the 'weighing of the heart'. This could be interpreted as literally as was desired.

The duo also saw new sights too, well, new old sights. The Colossus of Rhodes had been rebuilt, and the Hanging Gardens of Babylon never went away.

They worked a bit; they travelled a bit. Their travels led them to Italy, as they had always planned, and settled in Prato, Tuscany, where his mother had spent her childhood. Their lives became intertwined with the friends and relatives in the region. They ate and drank and told stories by candlelight. Luca was taught secret family recipes that varied only slightly from secret family recipes he had known before. Luca perfected his craft, whilst his father spent the end of his 23-years learning all he could about the early life of the woman he loved. "Let madre know I was here and let her know that I loved her." He would remind Luca from time-to-time.

When his father second-died Luca moved back to the Kingdom. He was sad to go but he had his own ties, and wanted to be there for his family should it come to pass, including his mamma.

"Luca," replied Michael warmly as he shook the man's hand "It's good to see you open. I've asked a friend to meet me here."
"Okay, but if he starts getting rowdy, he's for the door." Warned Luca.
"No, it's not Victor. A lady named Carol; you'll like her." Michael reassured Luca.
"And who is this?" Luca asked as he knelt to fuss the dog.
"This is 'Dog'", replied Michael "I'll make sure he behaves himself too." Michael took a seat near the back of the restaurant. It was early, but the

window seats were already taken. Once word got around that 'Luca Rossi' was open the place would be full to the rafters.

"Is your friend vegetarian or vegan?" There was no need for Luca to ask about intolerances or allergies as people on secondworld didn't have any. As well as there being no reservations or opening times, there was also no menu. This was not some avant-garde, bourgeoisie experiment. The lack of structure or choice was not put in place to create a buzz about the venue. It was infinitely more simplistic than that. This was commonplace for secondworld. You were not tied to anything unless you wanted to be. Luca opened when he wanted, and he cooked what he wanted. You came in, you sat down, and he would feed you. If you were vegetarian or vegan, Luca was more than happy to adapt the menu to accommodate, likewise with any religious restrictions. The payment was simple too. If you liked it, and could afford to, you left a little coin. If you wanted alcohol, unless Luca owed you a favour, you bought it.

Michael wasn't sure if Carol had any special requirements in relation to food but told Luca that he would ask her when she got here. He ordered a carafe of red wine for the table.

Carol arrived some time later in her usual shambolic manner. She had greeted Michael and was in her seat before she noticed the dog. The first she knew, something was snuffling around her legs. "God Almighty!" she exclaimed, followed by peals of laughter. She gave the dog the appropriate amount of attention, and then gave him some more.

Carol met Luca. They exchanged pleasantries and dietary requirements.

"I've just had a visit from the police." Carol announced when Luca had left. Michael felt a sudden flutter of adrenaline as is common when the police are mentioned and you have done nothing wrong.
"How come?" he asked.
"They're going door-to-door asking about the canal deaths." The term 'canal deaths' was coming into prominence. Carol went on to describe, in detail, the interaction between her and Jackie. "Well, that was all I could tell her about the scuffle, if that's what it even was, and that's all I can tell you about it too. It could have been something but was most probably nothing. People are always out doing stuff at all times of the day and night." Carol continued on, at times adding "Verbatim." To the end of a

relayed piece of dialogue that could not have possibly been said in that manner, or if it had, would have made for a very strange conversation. "She then pulled out a leather strap type thing; about yay big." Carol indicated the size of the strap with her index fingers. "It was pointed on one end and had like a loop on the other." Carol furrowed her brow. "Thing is, I've definitely seen it before, or something like it, but cannot for the life of me remember where." She looked Michael in the eye and raised and lowered her eyebrows dramatically.

"So, they think it's foul play then?" queried Michael.

"Yeah, I think so. It would have to be, wouldn't it? Bit odd if it wasn't? It's shook up some people from what I gather. They don't want to talk about it, acknowledge it even. It's okay for us, we're new. We're fresh from world-one, but people here are not used to this kind of thing." Carol paused when seeing Luca approach with two plates of steaming deliciousness.

"Pappardelle Al Ragu Di Cinghiale." Luca stated as he placed the food on the table. "Enjoy!" He smiled broadly and left the table. He was a sociable man but also knew not to outstay his welcome. The couple seemed to be deep in conversation and suspected they may have been talking in hushed tones about the canal deaths. These had unnerved him and he did not wish to be drawn in.

"Well, they haven't been out to see me yet, not that I'd be any use." Michael offered.

"Yeah. I mean, we keep saying they, I think it's just her really." Carol took a mouthful of her ragu followed by a slug of wine. She had underestimated the temperature of the food and needed to cool it down. "She seemed good though." Carol continued, after she managed to swallow her food. "Very thorough... Do you think she could help us?"

"What? With who murdered me?" said Michael.

"Who murdered us!" corrected Carol.

"No offence, but I think you've been involuntary manslaughtered." Joked Michael. Carol gave Michael a wry smile. "I doubt she'd be able to do much more than we're doing now." Continued Michael. "But it wouldn't hurt to ask, I suppose." Michael pushed a little bit of the meat to one side and scraped the sauce from it. He would give this to Dog under the table once he had finished his own.

Michael liked Carol. He liked her enthusiasm. She was treating his murder like some kind of 'Scooby do' mystery and he thought that given the circumstances, that was the correct amount of reverence for the matter. He was dead, but he was quite liking being dead. He did feel sorry for the losses that Carol had experienced though; the losses he had inadvertently caused. He felt she might need this murder mystery a little more than she would admit, but Michael was happy to entertain this, happy to be part of this welcome distraction for her.

By the end of the first course they had agreed to enlist Jackie into the investigation but only after getting a character reference from Victor. They would meet at Victors at 8am. If he was in agreement Carol would contact Jackie and arrange a meeting. She would not say what the meeting was about, just that she would like to talk to her. "She'll most probably think it's about the canal deaths, so she'll definitely turn up." Carol had stated, which prompted a brief discussion about the ethics of this tactic. "Look, we're only going to tell her the story. It's up to her whether she helps us or not. She might not be able to do anything anyway." Michael agreed to the terms whilst feeding pieces of meat to Dog "and after we have met with Jackie we can go and see if there is any news from the Bureau." Carol concluded.

Luca cleared the plates and continued with the courses. There was a type of cheese with pears and honey. There were all sorts of cured meat dishes that were enthusiastically introduced; "salame toscano"; "finocchiona"; "soppressata". There were breads and dips, and other accompaniments. Some came with a description, some came with a smile. All came with "Enjoy". And they did. At one point they were served with three "lardo di colonnata", a type of sausage; one for Carol, one for Michael and one for Dog. Though Dog was being adequately fed throughout the experience.

At the end of it all there was a sweet dark coffee and almond-based biscuits. Luca joined the couple at this stage and took in their company.

Declan Treanor

Michael and Carol bid their host farewell leaving behind them as much money as they had. They went their respective ways into the night fully sated and full with the richness of this life.

-

As Michael walked home, he became aware of someone behind him. Someone taking the same route as him. He was happy; he had a full belly and was contently inebriated. He saw no threat. He felt no danger. What he did feel was a sudden blow to the back of his head. He dropped to the ground.

The call

It was the phone that roused Jackie from her slumber on this occasion. She was not someone who was in the habit of oversleeping nor was her phone in the habit of receiving calls. Through bleary eyes and foggy thoughts, she picked up the receiver. "Hello. Jackie Taylor speaking." Those not accustomed to landlines generally didn't think to announce themselves but Jackie's previous experience on the force kicked in. "It's Carol. We met yesterday. Sorry it's so early but there have been some developments overnight and... and, I think I know what those bangles are."

The Falcon Man

Michael was woken by a wet nose. His head was still ringing from last night; partly from the wine but mostly from the almighty thump he had received. He could recall walking back from dinner and receiving a blow to the head. Michael was unsure if he lost consciousness, but it was certainly enough of an impact to cause Michael to fall to the ground and allow his assailant to push him into the canal. He remembered the impact on the back of his head and the impact of him hitting the water. Michael was unsure of how much information he had remembered and how much he had just pieced together.

He gasped and splashed in the canal and managed to grab hold of the bank. He thought he may have caught a glimpse of the figure running off but was unable to say this with any certainty. Michael got himself home, and after making sure all doors were locked and windows were shut, he took a shower. He dried himself and gave Dog some attention as he had been following Michael around since his return, unsure what to make of the events.
On drying his hair Michael felt the large lump on his head. It had grown in size, even since returning to the flat. Michael thought to himself that he just needed to sleep. He would sort this out in the morning, and the plan was to meet the police officer anyway. At least now they actually would have something to report.

The morning was now here, and he felt no need to deviate from the plan. He pulled on some clothes and dished out some food for Dog. He put some extra down as he was unsure when he would be back. Dog would not eat it all in one go as other dogs might, for some reason he always kept a little spare food in his bowl and would only eat this when his bowl was replenished, or it was time for bed. Michael was unsure what had caused this behaviour, but it seemed sensible enough. On leaving Michael propped the door ajar so the cur could come and go as it pleased. This was usual practice in secondworld, dogs were often left to roam the streets and it was only a problem if it was a problem. He would fit a doggy door soon, he thought to himself. Michael was unsure what they would be doing this morning and thought it best to not limit his options. "Good boy." He said as he fussed the hound. "You stay here. Go to bed. Good boy. Go to bed." Dog looked at him with puppy-dog eyes but reluctantly obeyed the order. Once he was stood in the dog bed his muscle memory kicked in and he curled up contented to settle to sleep for a while.

-

Michael made his way through the village and on to Victor's cabin. Whilst on his journey unbeknownst to him, his answerphone was picking up a message from the Bureau. Dog's ears pricked up at the sound of his master's voice then a high-pitched beep, followed by a strangers voice requesting that Michael call them back with "...the utmost urgency."

-

On arrival at the cabin Michael knocked on the door and called out "Victor!". There was no answer. He knocked again and still there was no reply. Michael was familiar enough with Victor to let himself in but decided to sit on the porch and wait. Soon enough the figure of Victor could be seen making his way through the trees. Michael stood up and waved to the man. The man stopped when he saw Michael, then held up his hand in reply and continued toward the cabin. The falcon arrived at the hut before Victor and perched atop the porch frame, eyeing Michael with caution.

"I thought Carol would be here. She not with you?" said Michael when Victor was in close enough range.
"She was, she left." Replied Victor.
Michael waited until Victor was just stepping on to the porch to continue the conversation "That's odd…. Did she say where she was going?"
Victor shook his head. "She said she wouldn't be too long and that we should wait here for her." Victor led the way into the small house.
"I wonder what that's about?" said Michael and followed Victor into the house. "Did she fill you in about the plan?" continued Michael.
"Not really, she was here then she went. She said she had to do something and would let us know when she got back. She won't be long." Victor replied.

"Okay, well we'll talk about it when she gets back then." conceded Michael and moved to change topic. "You missed a good night last night. It's a shame you couldn't make it."
"Well, he doesn't let me speak does he, that Luca one. Keeps telling me to be quiet." Victor retorted. "It was a good night, right up until someone hit me over the head and threw me in the canal." confessed Michael.
"What!?" replied Victor "Who did that then?"
"Suppose it was the same one who attacked the others. Stands to reason doesn't it. They have to treat them as murders now, don't they?" said Michael. Victor stood with his back to Michael busying himself with the stove and the kettle. Michael's eyes idly surveyed the walls of the cabin. As his eyes moved around the room Michael was drawn to several items in the corner hung on a thin wooden rail. Leather straps. He stepped closer to them. The leather straps were cut into a point at one end. They were cut at one end and curled at the other, some of them had bells attached. They had held no relevance previously but was this what Carol was talking about yesterday? She said she had seen them somewhere before. Was this where she saw them? Where was she now? He stepped closer still to the straps.

"What's this?" Michael picked up one of the leather strips. Victor turned to face Michael and looked at the falconry Jesses in his hands.
"It's okay." Victor raised up his palms and took a step towards Michael.
"Wait. What's okay? What are these? Where's Carol?"
"It's okay." Victor repeated. He took another step. "It's not what you think."
"So, what am I thinking? Why don't you tell me what I'm thinking!" Michael took a step back into the shelving that lined the wall.
"It doesn't have to go this way. I don't want to hurt you." Victor moved his right hand slowly but deliberately to the rear of his waistband; his left hand remained raised. When his hand reemerged a large hunting knife was in its grip. "But I will if I have to."

The cabin

Carol slid through the doorway, quickly assessing the situation she stepped in.
"Victor." she said softly. There was no reply. "Victor" she said slightly more firmly.
"Yup." Victor answered; he sounded the P with a pop.
"Victor, I've got someone here that needs to speak to Michael. Is that okay?" Carol cautiously sidled into the room, her eyes fliting from Michael whose eyes were fixed on Victor, to Victor holding Michael's gaze, to the blade in Victor's hand. "Is that okay Victor?" Carol's voice now stern "I have someone who wants to speak to Michael and I need to know everyone is going to be safe."

"Fine by me." Victor responded almost dismissively. He did not lower the knife.
"Come on in." Carol called to those outside the shack. Jackie stepped in through the door followed by a man that Victor did not recognise. Michael's eyes adjusted to light streaming into the once dimly lit cabin. "Darren?"

-

Michael's desire to embrace Darren was quelled by the form of a knife wielding Victor standing between them.

"Hello Michael." Said Darren, his voice steady.

"Darren, what are you doing here?" Michael's mind was reeling. "What is going on? They said you tried to kill me…that you did kill me."

Darren looked at Michael with something akin to pity in his eyes. "Michael, I did kill you. I didn't mean to hurt anyone else, but you needed to die."

Michael, suddenly faint, perched himself on the nearest ledge. He attempted to gather his thoughts but found them too disjointed, too disconnected. Partner aside, ultimately this was the man that killed Michael, and everyone else seemed very keen for them to be reunited.

"You needed to die Michael. You know that don't you?" Darren continued. "You understand that you needed to die." Darren left pauses for Michael to interject but Michael had no words. "You remember why you needed to die, don't you?... I found out... I found out about the killings."

Michael went to speak but could not. He searched for words of denial and incredulity, and none could be found. Instead, he found a fissure, a fracturing of the mind. Not quite memories, but the feelings that were tied to those memories. Michael spluttered "I can't... you didn't..." Then the images presented themselves. Bursts on a crimson canvass.

Flashes of horror came to him. He was still detached enough to realise that these were acts of depravity, but these were acts of depravity that he had committed. Blood. The terror of victims. He could not look away from this internal vision, though he longed for that more than anything. The screams of the ghosts of the past, only matched by the screams in his head. The taste of blood recalled. He retched at the thought.
Echoes of his crimes vied with the sins of his childhood.
The methodology was without distinction. Images of ropes, and knives; a hammer. Portraits of degeneracy invaded his mind.
He was looking at himself in a mirror, he was unsure of whose house it was. He was covered in blood. Just staring at himself. His focus shifted to the chair behind, viewed in the reflection, and the body slumped in that chair, still, other than the last pulses coming from the neck and cascading down the body.
Another image clicked in. A scene from above. The canal.
He was young. Too young. The door was locked. This was pushed to the side, like a slideshow projector, it pushed the image around the carousel and replaced it with a new horror. A Baroque masterpiece.

All his might could not stop this floodgate of memories. Misery after misery. How many had there been? He knew of course. The number twenty-one came to him, and he knew this to be true. Twenty-three murders, twenty-one victims. A rolodex of faces presented itself.

On that macabre roll call two of the faces came up twice. Florence and the twin.

23AM

A younger, more well-kept version of Victor.

I didn't mean to cause the crash — but I did mean to kill you.

Michael was aware of people talking around him.

A fugue state. Was that even possible? A thing of psychiatry myth and legend, psychological folk law.

All he ever did was build a cage for himself. Each kill merely strengthened the cage that held him. A cage for him, a grave for them.

He began to remember all of the things that he did. All of the horrible things. Abhorrent. He did not want to be that person.

It was like another him was sitting in the background. And he could now feel them

    in

        the

            back

                of

                    his

                        skull,

waiting to re-emerge, waiting to be reborn. He was no longer that person, but they were there. Every moment of recollection brought back more of the sense of that person. Would he become him again?

When he heard it, it made perfect sense to him.
Like a switch.

Declan Treanor

He could feel a latent hunger, he knew he could tap into if he so desired. He recognised it. Recognised a thirst for prey.

He knew that these memories he was now trying to quell; trying to vanquish; were once memories he savoured. He had held these memories dear, rolled them around his mouth….

…tasted them.

The line of keepsakes…

A garrotting with a piano wire. He had liked the idea of it, and the nostalgic element. He had purchased the wire and fashioned the two wooden handles before he was aware of who the victim would be.

A blood splattered hallway, the smell of bleach, a pursuit. Crimson. Purple. Blue. Muffled screams. Resistance, Scuffles. Muffled scuffles.

He had killed them because he had killed them before. He knew this was why they refused to acknowledge him. Deep down he knew this.

He felt grotesque.

Michael remembered walking to the cabin door. He did not stop. He was not stopped.

The Hidden

Would the cracks begin to show? Could man resist his nature. The petulance of existence. This is merely a blip. A celestial blink of an eye. Could the mask remain? If they had really changed it wouldn't be a mask, would it? Could they hold their newfound position? Like a sailor in a storm, holding the wheel and riding the waves. Pushing into the swells. Trying to maintain the course, trying to weather the storm. Ignoring the claps of thunder, ignoring the water lapping on to the deck and down through the cabin. Those secrets we don't admit to others, those we don't admit to ourselves. Those left festering in the deepest parts of us, that will rot us from the inside out. Could these still be a part of us, or are they gone?

In the grand tapestry of existence, where the threads of change wove a complex pattern, questions lingered like unspoken echoes in the corridors of the mind. Would the cracks begin to show, revealing the vulnerabilities that hid beneath the façade of resilience? Could man resist his nature, that intrinsic pull toward both creation and destruction?

There is a hidden way, a hidden path, but it is in plain sight. It sits before us, it reminds us of its presence but we do not see it, or see it ever so briefly that it remains elusive. A furtive glance from a familiar friend. We think we recognise it but cannot picture it. We believe ourselves mistaken. We carry on with our lives.

The thought of it was never as bad as the deed itself. Was that true? Surely the thought was the all of it. Actions are but a mechanism, the thoughts are what save us or defeat us. If we do something that we believe just, or convince ourselves just, the actions are nothing. If we do something that we will not allow ourselves to reconcile, then it cannot be reconciled. The torment is of our own making. Even if our actions lead to consequences, we can bear these if we believe ourselves to be righteous, or at the very least, not unnatural.

Declan Treanor

Thoughts, after all, are the architects of our actions, the silent orchestrators of the narratives that unfold in our lives.

A bell unrung.

Actions, it was reasoned, are but mechanisms driven by the engine of thought. The real power lies in the realm of ideas, convictions, and ethical considerations. If we undertake an action we deem just, or successfully convince ourselves of its justice, the deed itself becomes a mere manifestation of the underlying thought. In this light, actions are nothing more than the outward expressions of our inner convictions.

Conversely, if we engage in an action that we cannot reconcile with our beliefs or values, the torment that ensues is of our own making. The disparity between our actions and our internal moral compass creates a dissonance that reverberates through the very core of our being. Even if these actions lead to external consequences, the burden is most palpably borne within the chambers of our conscience.

The power of belief, the ability to convince oneself of the righteousness or, at the very least, the neutrality of one's actions, becomes a crucial element in navigating the complexities of morality and consequence. The internal dialogue, the negotiation between thought and action, shapes the narrative of our lives. In this interplay, the adage is challenged, and the true weight of deeds is found not in the actions themselves but in the fertile soil of thought from which they spring.

The rub is when you are not able to convince yourself. You have not shored up the correct psychological stronghold. A Faraday cage for the neural pathways. Some way to stem the intrusive thought that you are flawed.

The petulance of existence, a stubborn insistence on the unpredictable, whispered through the cosmic winds. This moment, this ephemeral blip in the celestial timeline, held the weight of a universe's gaze. Yet, it was merely a blip, a celestial blink of an eye, a fleeting passage in the vast expanse of time.

A table with items of significance. Move away and the significance wanes. Pan out. A house, a street. As the lens of perspective widened, the scene unfolded from the confines of a single house to the expanse of an entire street. Pan out further, the view capturing the mosaic of lives interconnected within the neighbourhood. Yet, the questions lingered, echoing across the vastness of existence.

How many other forced lives existed within this intricate tapestry of humanity? Did it matter? Now at a cosmic distance, observed the microscopic struggles and triumphs, the joys and sorrows, of each individual existence. From this perspective, the significance of each life seemed to diminish, a mere blip in the grand scheme of the universe.

How many people found themselves painted into a corner, their choices and opportunities limited by circumstances beyond their control? The universality of this predicament. Did it apply to all of them, all of us? The concept of limited choice became an existential inquiry, transcending the boundaries of the scene before it.

In this vast cosmic ballet, the individual struggles of a street, a city, or even a planet seemed to fade into the cosmic background. Yet, within each life, there existed a universe of experiences, emotions, and narratives that defied cosmic indifference. The panorama of existence, viewed from the distance of the cosmos, paradoxically emphasized the profound significance of every individual story against the backdrop of the infinite.

The earth will explode in 8 billion years. This is a mighty distance. But each year it becomes closer. A certainty. There is no escaping this fact. Life will find a way. Yes, life will find a way. Naivety or arrogance leads us to believe this life will be us.

We are monsters- time will judge us so. Electrified bags of fat and meat; bone and spittle.

Declan Treanor

Scrabbling around, trying to find something to do. Trying to find meaning in a life that is ultimately banal. Take the most splendid, the most magnificent human being you can think of. How are you and they separated? There is not much in it. What will be thought of this spectacular human in 5'000 years. What would be thought of them in 100 years, or 50? What are they to the mind of a blue whale? Nothing. Two planets collide and not an eyelid is batted. Ice giant exoplanets collide creating a blaze of light visible 1'800 light-years away. An actor wears a t-shirt.

The sea

Michael looked out to the sea.

He had left Victor's shack that day and just continued to walk. They had let him go, perhaps as they were sure what he would ultimately do. He had walked out of the village and just kept walking. He found hedgerows to sleep in. No undue attention was brought to him, people were used to walkers. This was the norm, not an oddity. He had not thought to bring anything with him but sated his hunger by drinking from streams.

He thought briefly about his dog but was confident that someone would look after him.

Passing through one town he allowed himself some soup which he paid for by trading his jacket. An unbalanced trade but Michael was happy to do so. The vendor gave the soup for free. This was secondworld after all, and the vendor's decency had not been eroded by greed. Michael sat and chatted with the vendor. This was the first interaction he had since leaving the shed two days ago, other than a nod of the head to acknowledge another's greeting. The conversation was, on the surface, superficial but it was wrapped in warmth and kindness, and it made Michael feel good. He questioned briefly whether he had the right to feel good but concluded that this pilgrimage was not a penance.

He had enjoyed the Welsh coast as a child, but it was not until adulthood that he came to truly appreciate it. He guessed he was somewhere between Colwyn Bay and Prestatyn but didn't quite know where. It was not somewhere he immediately recognised. He considered asking someone where he was or maybe walk along the coast until he came across some signpost or a map, but he didn't suppose it mattered either way.

Looking out into the crashing waves he knew that God was in those waters. Those waters that stretched out to the horizon. Whales blew in the distance, orca's frolicked nearby. He felt at peace. Both sides of him. The man reborn and the monster inside. They looked out at the sea together and it quietened their soul.

Declan Treanor

Michael spent some time like this, watching the sea. He sat down on the large rocks that bordered the beach. He was not nervous, not rethinking what needed to come, he was wondering at the majesty of life while he still could. Then, as the light began to hint at its retreat he stood. He undressed, folding his clothes and placing them on the rock beside him. Michael gave an involuntary shiver. It would soon be winter. He walked purposefully across the sand and into the water.

The waves crashed about his legs, enveloping and grasping at different parts of him in icy cold water as the sea ebbed and flowed and he strode forward. His jaw juddered with the cold, but he strode on regardless. He walked until it was deep enough for him to swim. As he swam the cold retreated into the background.

He knew he would grow tired soon, too tired to make it back. What was next? Was there a world three? Terra Incognita. A world where the memories were buried deeper still. A world where he had a real chance to be a different person, devoid of the need to kill. Did he deserve such a chance? Maybe not.

Returning to stardust, beyond morality or desire. Joining those he had destroyed. Joining all things.

Michael began to panic. He felt fear grip him. He searched for the monster. His other self joined him again for the final moments. Michael was calmed by this, knowing that he had to take the other to their watery grave. He found comfort and solace in the other. They became as one. They knew that their aching limbs would soon bring relief. Relief from the pain they had inflicted on others, the burden they carried. The dark water took him. The dark took the other. Their lungs burnt as they sank. They had finally reached the end.

The end.

Autumn's Mantra

And Autumn's mantra is next year. Always next year.

Next year I will change.

Next year things will be different.

Next year.

Prologue

Did he really think that they were going to let him just walk out? Was he stupid? Did he think they were stupid? When Michael left the cabin Jackie went with him. This was one of the scenarios they had covered on the morning, before confronting Michael.

Jackie had received a call from Carol in the early hours. She said that she remembered seeing some leather straps in her friend Victor's cabin, the same leather straps found on the bodies of the ones found by the canal. She then went on to tell Jackie about Michael, his murder and his husband. At that time Carol was at the Bureau. She informed Jackie that Darren had now entered secondworld, that he was being held for Michael's murder, but that he was making some pretty wild allocations.

Jackie went to the Bureau. Darren had found out that Michael was killing people, that he had been for years. Darren had killed Michael and then killed himself whilst in custody awaiting trial.

They argued about what needed to be done. Michael was a different person now- well, not if he killed the ones found by the canal. We could just arrest him- you could just arrest him. This was a very straightforward world-one solution, one that did not sit well with Jackie. "They will use this. They will use this to scare people, and to take back the power they had in world-one." She could see it now. Innocent was happy to ignore the murders at the canal, but if his hand was forced Jackie was in no doubt that he would allow the situation to be exploited, especially if he was to gain from it.

"He needs to die." Jackie did not mince her words. The three had been left alone in a room unguarded; after all, Jackie was a police officer, the only police officer they had. Carol and Darren looked at each other and then avoided eye contact with Jackie. "You know I'm right." She waited in silence until Darren met her eye. "You've already been through this Darren. Sometimes you have to take matters into your own hands." "But at what price?" Darren whispered. "I killed him and couldn't live with myself after."

After further discussion it was agreed. If there was an altercation, they would defend themselves. This defence of self would need to result in the second-death of Michael. If he did not attack them, they would let him go and Jackie would follow him to see what he did. They thought, given the circumstances, he may try to take his life. This would be preferable.

There was a third option, known to Jackie and suspected by the others, but not spoken. Jackie was resolute that this man would not harm anyone again. She would follow, and she would wait, but there is only so much waiting someone can do.

Darren was released to Jackie under her authority and a phone call was made to Victor. He was told that Michael was coming over and that he needed to stall him. He was told that Michael was dangerous and a brief history of what they knew was given. Victor did not seem surprised. Jackie had wondered how long Victor had known the truth.

So, when he left Jackie tracked him. She thought to herself that the old him would have seen her, but this was a man dejected. She camped as he did, but always taking the higher ground. She called in to Carol every evening. She carried with her a means of dispatch. He would be dead soon, one way or another.

She watched him on the shoreline. Had he changed his mind? No, he would do the decent thing. Most people in this world did. Even serial killers. She watched as he took himself out into the ocean. She watched until she could no longer see him. Then she watched some more.

Printed in Great Britain
by Amazon